DAVID A. POULSEN

THE DARK WON'T WAIT

Red Deer Press

Published in Canada by Red Deer Press,
209 Wicksteed Avenue, Unit 51, Toronto, ON   M4G 0B1.

Published in the United States by Red Deer Press,
60 Leo M Birmingham Pkwy, Ste 107, Brighton, MA 02135.

Red Deer Press acknowledges with thanks the Canada Council for the Arts and the Ontario Arts
Council for their support of our publishing program. We acknowledge the financial support of the
Government of Canada through the Canada Book Fund (CBF) for our publishing activities.

Library and Archives Canada Cataloguing in Publication
Title: The dark won't wait / David A. Poulsen.
Names: Poulsen, David A., 1946- author.
Identifiers: Canadiana 20240400593 | ISBN 9780889957602 (softcover)
Subjects: LCGFT: Novels.
Classification: LCC PS8581.O848 D37 2024 | DDC jC813/.54—dc23

Publisher Cataloging-in-Publication Data (U.S.)
Names: Poulsen, David A., 1946- author.
Title: The dark won't wait / David A. Poulsen.
Description: Toronto, Ontario: Red Deer Press, 2024. | Summary: Dom Cantrell's life
revolves around high school, cars, and baseball until his attraction to an elusive girl--
and a local murder--turn his world upside-down." – Provided by publisher.
Identifiers: ISBN 978-0-88995-760-2 (paperback)
Subjects: LCSH: High school boys – Juvenile fiction. | Murder – Investigation –
Juvenile fiction. | Hate crimes – Juvenile fiction. | BISAC: YOUNG ADULT FICTION
/ Boys & Men. | YOUNG ADULT FICTION / Thrillers & Suspense / Crime. | YOUNG
ADULT FICTION / Law & Crime.
Classification: LCC PR9199.3.P635 Dar 2024 | DDC 813/.54 – dc23

Edited for the Press by Beverley Brenna
Text and cover design by Tanya Montini
Printed in Canada by Copywell

www.reddeerpress.com

DAVID A. POULSEN

THE
DARK
WON'T
WAIT

To all the kids in all the schools I have visited through the years. Talking to and with you guys about books and stories and writing is the very best part of being a writer. And to my youngest grandkids—Dillan, Chloe, Gabriella and Eva.

1

FEBRUARY 16TH

———————

The Girl in the Window

I hate this car.

For starters it's a Plymouth Reliant Station Wagon. But that's not the bad part. No, the bad part, the really, really bad part is that it's a *1981* Plymouth Reliant Station Wagon. That makes the car forty-two years old.

My mom is only two years older than the car.

Original paint. That's normally a good thing—you see it in car ads, a selling point. Not with the station wagon. The aging green paint was once the colour of leaves but now is the colour of *dead* leaves. Oh, and it has that lovely fake wood along the sides that was all the rage back when Richie Cunningham and the Fonz were cruising on TV. And don't give me that—*it's a classic car... must be worth some serious cash.* Yeah, right. You notice the first syllable in the word classic. Right ... class. Now, maybe there's a 1981 Plymouth Reliant Station Wagon out there that *is* a classic car. But I'm betting that car does not exhale blue-black smoke and make a rattling sound that Tuesdays, Thursdays and Saturdays comes from the left side of the car and the rest of the week magically migrates to my side, the passenger side—somewhere between my right knee and the right front fender.

And that *actual* classic car probably doesn't have an interior smell that is a blend of overworked, under-washed sweat socks, decaying dog crap and burnt popcorn. I'll take the blame for the socks but we don't have a dog and I don't ever remember having popcorn in the car so I can't explain those except to say that maybe the car is also haunted ... by the ghost of a popcorn-loving Welsh Corgi. I call it the Satan Wagon because it really is the car from Hell.

All of which is why, now that I'm in high school, I insist that Mom drop me off a block from the school at the corner of Hastings Road and Child Avenue. Although the fact that I emerge from a billowing blue cloud at the same place and at almost the same time every school morning might have blown my cover.

Today is just another day of car hate—nothing special about it. Until we stop to fill up at McCloy's Rapid Fuel. If I hadn't known what day it was, I would now. Because Mom stops at McCloy's every Wednesday morning. Mom is a creature of habit—if you're Libby Cantrell you drive the same car for a couple of decades and you fuel that car at the same place on the same day every week. It's like I'm living the movie Groundhog Day except worse because of the car.

Of course, Libby isn't actually her name—in the same way Dom isn't my name. She's Elizabeth and I'm Dominic but both of those names are just too much work. So Libby and Dom it is.

Mom likes to handle the filling of the car herself so usually I check my phone or maybe knock off a page or two of whatever book I'm reading. But today, maybe because it's already mid-summer warm outside, even though it's only the middle of February, or maybe to escape the car's interior aroma which is a little more intense on warm days, I set my book down and step outside of the car.

McCloy's is between the street—Hastings Road— and the alley and because Mom is at the far right-hand pump, we're closer to the alley than the street.

I stretch, then I take a few steps, kind of to get the kinks out, and I smile. Because today, even though I'm being driven to school in that car, I'm in a really good mood. I'm not sure why except that it's an amazing morning—one of those mornings that fills you with optimism about how the rest of the day is going to go.

I see two little kids, boys maybe nine or ten and they're playing catch in the back alley. Playing catch in February. That's how unseasonably warm it's been. And they're working their way—slowly—toward their school, the elementary school. My smile gets bigger as I watch them throw the ball back and forth three or four times, then take maybe two steps in the direction of school, then some more catch. I love their attitude—no sense rushing that whole getting-to-school thing.

One of them misses the ball and it rolls over to where I am. I pick it up and toss it to the kid who missed it and he grins at me.

"Can you throw us a high sky?"

"A high sky?"

He points up in the air.

"Oh, a high sky," I say. "Sure."

He tosses me the ball and I throw it up in the air.

David A. Poulsen

Neither of them comes close to catching it. The kid who threw me the ball holds his glove awkwardly, making it pretty well impossible to catch something coming down at him. I walk over and show him.

"Try that."

I pick up the ball and throw another "high sky." Not too high this time. The kid I helped makes the catch and grins at me like he just made the final out in game seven of the World Series. I grin back at him and wave. I figure I better get back to the beater. Mom's probably got it filled.

That's when I see her. No, not her. *Her.* She's at the window of a house across the alley from the gas station and she's looking in my direction. Watching me? Smiling at me? I'm not sure. Too far away to be certain of the expression on her face. Besides, even if she is smiling it's probably not at me.

It's likely the *kitchen* window. And I smile back at her and start to give a little wave. But I don't finish it. What if she's not really smiling at me? She'll think I'm an idiot. I look behind me and there's no one there for her to be smiling at. So maybe it *is* me.

She looks about my age but I'm sure I haven't seen her before. I'm in my second year at Hastings Park High but it's a big school, I think around 900 kids, so there's lots of them I still don't know—probably a few I've never even seen yet. And if she goes to Walter Webster, the K–8 school, or the Catholic high school, Monsignor Irvine, well, then I might never have seen her.

Until today. I look back toward the car and as I thought, Mom has finished filling it and is looking around for me. I take one last glance at the house but the girl in the window is gone. So I can't be sure if she was actually smiling at me. I guess it doesn't really matter all that much, but it would be nice to know. You know, to go along with my good mood.

I memorize the house which is kind of stupid but I do it anyway. Light blue siding, older bungalow, likely built in the sixties or seventies ... probably two bedrooms on the main floor, L-shaped living-dining room, detached garage. I know more about houses than most fifteen-year-olds do because my mom is a realtor and I've had to spend way too many Saturdays, and some Sundays too, bored out of my mind on my iPad in somebody else's house while Mom showed it to people. I'm especially good with bungalows of that vintage which seem to be the ones my mom is often selling.

I wouldn't want her job but she has to do something, especially since Dad died two years ago. Mom always says she'd hate to work in an office, so I guess the realtor thing works for her. And other than the boring Saturdays and Sundays, it sort of works okay for me too. Mom is home for dinner most nights and she does her best to get to my hockey games in winter and baseball games in summer. I have to say I've got most of the stuff I want—it's not like we're poor or anything. And hey, look at how good I am at figuring out what the inside of the mystery girl's house looks like. A skill like that, you never know when it will come in handy. Yeah, right. Maybe if I become a realtor too and that is *not* going to happen.

Back in the Satan Wagon, I try to get my mind on something else but I've already got a plan cooked up in my head. After school, I'll jump on my bike and ride back over to McCloy's, maybe grab a bag of chips or something so that, in case the kitchen girl's watching, it doesn't look like she's the reason I'm in the neighbourhood.

Then I'll ride up and down the alley a few times and who knows, I might even glance over that way, toward the house with the light blue siding. You know, just in case.

2

FEBRUARY 16TH – LATER

Good Day-Bad Day

Okay, so much for all that optimism I was feeling this morning.

I'm sitting in math staring at a test Mr. Gonzales handed back a few minutes ago. It's my worst mark of the year—54%. But what really sucks is that I was sure I had aced this one ... well, maybe not aced exactly, but somewhere in the 70–80% range. My mark is like the Plymouth Reliant Station Wagon of math marks. And it doesn't help that my two besties—Farhad Shirvani and Mia Stark— both did way better than I did. Farhad pulled down a 76% and Mia, who I'm pretty sure is a closet genius, rocked an 84%.

I'd rather stick pins in my eyes than repeat Grade 10 math but a few more grades like this one and another ten months with Mr. Gonzales could be a reality.

So now I'm pouting and counting down the final minutes to the end of the school day. Then it's get home, climb on my bike and ride down the alley by McCloy's to see if the girl who may or may not have been smiling at me this morning is back at her kitchen window.

But even after the end-of-day song plays—this week it's Harry Styles's "As It Was"—racing off for home isn't the first thing that happens. No, that's because every day after school, Mia, Farhad and I meet at this cool metal park bench just outside the front doors of the school. When I say "cool," I don't mean cool as in neat or awesome or amazing. No, I mean cool as in cold. On winter days the metal is at least ten degrees colder than the actual temperature outside. I don't understand the science of that—all I know is that it is very uncomfortable on the butt and we sit on binders, hoodies, whatever we've got that can keep our backsides from actually making contact with the ass-freezing iron of the bench. Farhad says we're all going to get hemorrhoids but that doesn't stop us from gathering in the same location almost every day.

But today, that's not a problem. I mentioned it's

February; it's also the warmest day of winter so far, so our bums are safe from frostbite (and hemorrhoids) as we sit down to recap and dissect our day. Not that we talk about stuff that happened in class—that would be totally geeky; no, actually, we discuss just about everything else. Some might call it a gossip session and I guess it sort of is.

Farhad's main interest is girls—so he leads off with a summary of his exploits in that regard—*Sue Cole smiled at me; I'm pretty sure Jacqueline Rotheslear wants to ask me to ask her out; Sandy Yu told me she wished her handwriting looked like mine.* There's more—there always is—but Mia and I quickly lose interest and are soon looking around at kids getting into their parents' cars, birds hopping around on the patches of the lawn that aren't snow-covered, and a couple of Grade 12 guys who are tossing a Frisbee back and forth and are pretty good at it.

Mia is too polite to interrupt but the instant Farhad stops to take a breath she jumps in.

"The Drama Club is having auditions Friday at noon ... I'm thinking of going just to see what's happening."

She tries to sound casual because last year she was totally sure she would get the lead in *Anne of Green*

David A. Poulsen

Gables. She was pretty choked when she didn't. In fact, not only did she not get the Anne part, she didn't even get the best friend part. What she got was the busybody old lady who lives up the road from Green Gables. I actually thought she was really funny in that role but Mia was still angry after the play's performances were over and swore she was done with "the theatre."

Now here we are a year later, and it looks like maybe there's been a change of heart.

"What play are they doing this year?" I ask, keeping it light, leaving her the option of saying, *Oh some English thing, doesn't sound very interesting.*

"*Wait Until Dark,*" she says. "Might be okay, I suppose." She's trying even harder than I am to keep it all calm and uninterested but I'm not fooled.

"*Wait Until Dark!*" Farhad has actually come to life and practically yells it. "That was like the scariest movie ever. They're doing that play at our school? I might even go see it. You should try out for sure."

Mia shrugs, yawns, tries to look bored. "I don't know. I'll have to see. I'm pretty busy from now until the end of the school year."

"Really?" I look at her. "Doing what?"

She glares at me. Mia doesn't like to be questioned or argued with. "Grade 10 is kind of important, you know ... Mister Fifty-four Percent. I've got to get good grades the rest of high school so I can get a scholarship to a school that actually matters as opposed to City College."

Wow, she gets off two nasty shots in one spiel—the 54% thing and the City College reference. She knows that's where I'll probably be going. And City is considered the school you go to if a real university won't take you. Nasty and nasty.

But even if I wanted to return fire, there's no time. Farhad's dad pulls up in front of the school and we bail off the bench and head for the car, a 2018 Audi Q7, pretty much the other end of the vehicle spectrum from the Satan Wagon. Our parents trade off providing rides home for us and this is Mr. Shirvani's week. I'm quiet all the way home, a little sulky, I admit it. *Mister Fifty-four Percent.* That one hurt but I figure in the car with Farhad's dad driving (and listening), I'm not going to make it an issue. Besides, Mia's probably just nervous and tense about the auditions so I'll give her a pass this time.

I'm the first one dropped off. I give one quick wave in the direction of the departing Audi and its occupants

David A. Poulsen

and then head for the house. Surely the day is about to get better. In the front door, I drop the books off, check the note on the kitchen table ... *Hey Sweetie, I have a showing this afternoon, can you turn the oven to 350 at about five o'clock, your favourite casserole, love you ... Mom,* then through the house, a stop at the fridge for a fast glass of orange juice, and out into the backyard to grab my bike.

The sky is that forever-blue you get some days and it's still warm outside so the ride back to McCloy's helps me forget my less-than-great day at school. By the time I turn into the McCloy's lot, I'm back to smiling. I run into the service station for a Slurpee, then roll into the back alley stopping at about the same place I was this morning. No kids playing catch this time.

And no girl looking out the window of the bungalow with the light blue siding. I guess I was kind of stupid to expect it. Like she's been standing there all day hoping the guy who got out of the smoke-belching station wagon would come by again. Duh.

I finish the Slurpee and head down the alley, noting that her house is the fourth one from the corner. I circle the block to ride by the front of the house. Just in case she's standing out front or maybe looking out the living room window.

Four houses along I slow down and pretend I'm having trouble with my chain. Yeah, that would fool anyone. I look over at the house—624 Edmond Avenue. I have a pretty good view of the interior through the large living-room window. I nod to myself as I realize I pretty much nailed the layout of the place this morning. Large living room window to the left, leading to the kitchen at the back of the house and the window where I'd seen her. A hallway accessible from the dining area and the kitchen that leads to two bedrooms and a bathroom. Stairs from the back of the kitchen, going down three or more stairs to the back door or if you make a right turn, more stairs leading down to the basement.

What I can't know, of course, is whether there have been any renovations (*upgrades* in real-estate-speak) or if the basement is developed. The two small windows just above the foundation aren't about to reveal that information. The front yard is well kept—a couple of flower beds waiting patiently to come to life for another year, some nice shrubs and one large, healthy-looking spruce tree with last year's Christmas lights still in place.

David A. Poulsen

I fuss with the chain for a few more minutes, realize that people have replaced both tires in the time it's taking me to deal with my chain "problem," and ride on. I make a couple of casual looks back and give up. The mystery girl is nowhere to be seen.

Actually, the house looks empty, like there's no one home. Trust me to run a stakeout on an empty house.

Talk about a roller-coaster day. The Satan Wagon to kick it off (bad), the girl in the window (good), the 54% math test (bad), gorgeous day for a bike ride (good), no girl in the window (bad) and there are still five or six hours left until lights out at the house of Cantrell.

———————————

3

The Non-Audition

"You should come," Mia says. "They never have enough guys for all the parts and there are some really good ones in this play."

I was barely in the door after my Edmund Avenue drive-by when she phoned. She almost always texts so when I saw her number on caller I.D., I figured this had to be important.

"There's all these bad guys—drug smugglers, killers—you'd be perfect."

I wonder if that's meant as a compliment, decide it doesn't matter. "I'm not an actor." I say the words slowly for emphasis. "The biggest part I ever played was an egg in our Grade 2 class play for the parents. I don't think I was very good. All I had to do was push the top off the egg and climb out. But it got stuck and both me and the egg tipped over. At which point I started crying and the teacher, Miss Pargeter, had to come out on stage and rescue me. My dad told me I got the biggest laugh of the whole play. I told him that wasn't really the point; the egg wasn't a comedy role—I knew that much even in Grade 2. And I've never been in any plays since, not even the Christmas pageant at the church. I think I'll keep my record intact."

"Okay, then why don't you just come out and be there for me. I'm totally nervous and it would be really helpful if I knew there was one person there who was pulling for me."

"Even if that person only managed 54% on his math test?" I'm kind of reluctant to let that go.

"Hey, I'm sorry," Mia says. "That was a bitch thing to say and I feel bad. Honestly. Please come to the auditions. *Please.* Besides you never know—there could be this amazing omelet part that they'll want somebody with egg experience to play."

We both laugh at that but I tell her only that I'll think about it.

Which unleashes a barrage of texts that go on most

of the evening. Promises of cookies, help with math, and even a pledge to come to at least one of my baseball games which is big because Mia hates baseball. Finally at 9:57 PM I agree to go with her mostly because I'm sick of listening to the ping on my phone every three or four minutes.

The texts stop then and I abandon my unfinished homework in favour of a shower and bed with a book.

I've never been to an audition before—I got the egg part because every kid in the class was already cast as someone/something else—so for a while it's interesting. Eight girls read for the role of Suzy Hendrix who is blind. After the third or fourth girl I kind of lose interest and am playing with my phone. I almost miss Mia's audition but look up just in time.

She sits on one of the two chairs at the front of the stage. She's sitting next to a Grade 11 guy named Foster MacLennan. He's reading the part of Mike, a guy who's a crook but doesn't seem like a totally bad guy. Foster has read the part of Mike with all eight girls—nine counting Mia—so I'm assuming he's pretty much a lock

David A. Poulsen

to play that part. And I have to say he's really good. I've seen him around the school, but don't really know the guy. He comes across as someone who thinks he's pretty amazing, but that's probably unfair since, like I said, I don't really know him.

A couple of the girls who have read for Suzy were pretty good too so I'm a little worried that Mia hasn't got much of a shot. She's kind of nervous with the first few lines and it shows but after that she rolls along pretty well and I'm thinking she might at least have a chance.

Then the drama teacher, Miss Kerver, does something she didn't do with any of the other girls. She asks Mia to get up out of the chair and walk back maybe ten steps. Then she says, "Okay, Mia, you're blind. You know there's a chair right next to where Mike is sitting but you can't see it, of course. I want you to walk to the chair as a blind person would."

I'm thinking, *Holy crap that's tough,* but Mia nods and turns her back to the audience where I'm sitting, then she turns again to face us. And she's blind. Seriously. She's suddenly this woman trying to get to that chair and for a second I'm sure she's going to miss it and maybe walk off the stage and break several bones but then she reaches out and feels the chair. But she doesn't just relax and sit down—she's still feeling with her hands where the seat is and everything and when she finally gets sat down, Miss Kerver and I both applaud.

Now I'm thinking Mia has aced it and that's when things go horribly wrong. Miss Kerver says, "Okay, I need someone to read the part of Carlino, another of the bad guys and Mike's pal."

She looks around the theatre so I do too. And she and I undoubtedly realize at about the same time that there is only one male in the place other than Foster up there on stage. That guy is me.

"I guess you're up next," Miss Kerver says to me.

I shake my head so hard I think for a minute I might have dislocated my neck. "I'm ... I'm not here to audition. I'm just watching."

"Nonsense," she says firmly, hands on her hips as if to say, *Don't mess with me, boy.* "This is an audition. If you come to auditions, you must be here to audition. It's right there in the drama rulebook."

Now both of us know there is no drama rulebook and I'm pretty sure not everyone at an audition is there to audition. But words fail me right at that moment so

I just shake my head one more time and hold up my phone—I have no idea why.

"You can't phone in the audition." She smiles and I fumble my phone into my pocket. "But hey I can't force you."

Right! I want to yell but I just nod instead, thinking (and hoping) this horrible moment in my life is coming to an end. I'm wrong because at that exact second Farhad comes walking out onto the stage from the area to the side. He's grinning and pointing.

"Come on, Dom, at least read the thing so Mike can get a feel for his character. You'd really be helping out and this way if there's a scene later where we need an egg, we know who to call."

First of all I'm wondering how he knows about my egg disaster. I'm pretty sure I never mentioned it to him. And secondly ...

"We? What we? What are you talking about? Are you part of this too?"

He bows. "Farhad Shirvani, Sound and Lights Production Coordinator, at your service."

And then Mia's there beside him. "Just a few lines, Dom. To help Mike out."

I look over at Mike. He looks bored with the whole thing. I don't think he cares if I read the part of Carlino or not. He's staring at the ceiling—probably thinking about dating Becky G and Mackenzie Foy after he becomes famous.

I slowly get to my feet and begin a zombie shuffle to the stage hoping that the school will be evacuated due to a volcano alert in the next thirty seconds. There's a set of steps at one corner of the stage so I climb up and stop in front of Miss Kerner. She smiles and hands me a script.

"Page 31," she says and she leans forward. "Thank you, I really appreciate this." She says it like it's our secret. But I'm onto her devilish plan. It's all part of a plot to suck me into the play. *Yeah, well good luck. I'll read a few lines to help out Mike here and that's it.*

Miss Kerver goes down the stairs and takes a seat in the first row. I sit down next to Foster MacLennan.

He looks at me, doesn't say anything.

"Hey," I say and he nods.

"So how do you want to play this?" he asks me.

What the hell does that mean? "Um ... I don't know ... what do you think?"

"Well, Mike's the smarter of the two guys and kind of the leader, except for Roat, of course, so I think you wanna play him tough but a little insecure, you know, like he kind of looks up to Mike and pretty much follows him on everything."

"Yeah ... uh ... right, that's what I was thinking too."

Which is totally stupid. First of all, I know nothing about Carlino; I've never heard of Roat; and I have exactly zero idea about playing the guy "tough but a little insecure. Where's that damn volcano evacuation warning anyway?

He reads a line. I look down at the page. I can't find that line anywhere. I say nothing.

Finally, after a silence that goes well past uncomfortable, Miss Kerver intervenes. "That's an interesting way to play him, but we already have a character in this play who is blind," she says. "And I'm not aware of Carlino being deaf. I think I'd prefer it if you'd just go ahead and read the line that's written."

"I ... yes ... I ..."

Foster leans over and hisses. "*Thirty*-one. You're on page twenty-one."

I fumble through the pages, find the right one but

I'm not confident I can read the line because I'm pretty sure I'm mere seconds from passing out.

Foster (Mike) reads his line again—it's something about a doll with heroin hidden inside. And this time I'm ready. And even though I'm a little shaky to start with, I figure I more or less nail it ... and most of the lines after that.

We finish reading the scene and Foster gives me a half-hearted fist bump. And Miss Kerver applauds. Although I have the feeling that maybe what I see on her face is mostly relief.

"You did that very well ... uh ... Don."

"Dom."

"What?"

"It's Dom," I explain. "It's short for Dominic."

"I'm sorry." She shakes her head. "Dom. Have you acted before?"

I clear my throat, playing for time. "Well, there was one—"

"Yes, he has, Miss Kerver." Mia cuts me off, apparently feeling that a recounting of the egg fiasco could be career threatening. "Dom has been in plays before. I saw him—he's really good."

A bald-faced lie. And I'm hoping Miss Kerver doesn't follow up with the obvious question: *So, Dom, what plays have you been in?*

"Well, as I said, you were very good, Dom, and I'd like to offer you the role of Carlino."

I look around the theatre wondering where all the other actors are who are trying out for that part. But, of course, nobody else has magically showed up so Foster and Farhad are the only other males in the place. Foster is already cast and Farhad is the sound and lights guy. That leaves me.

"Well, uh ... actually, Miss Kerver, like I said, I'm not here to audition for the play. I'm Mia's friend and I just came to support her, sort of cheer her on." I hope my grin doesn't *look* as stupid as it feels.

"Dom, here's the thing." Miss Kerver climbs slowly up on stage and stands in front of Foster and me—both of us still sitting in the chairs. Well, actually Foster is pretty much sprawled in his chair looking beyond bored. I'm sitting up straight in mine; my guess is I'm looking terrified.

Miss Kerver's voice is softer than most teachers' voices. "I'd really like to do this play. I think it could be amazing—one of the best things the drama club has ever done here at Hastings. But there are four parts for men and I don't have enough male actors. Specifically I don't have anyone for Carlino and you just hit a home run in your reading. But without you, there is no Carlino, no *Wait Until Dark*, no drama production at all this year."

"I'm really sorry, Miss Kerver, but I just can't. Baseball season will be starting"— actually, practices won't start for a month and a half, but I'm hoping she doesn't know that—"so I'd have to miss rehearsals and—"

"We rehearse over the noon hour right up until the last week when we'll have run-throughs and dress rehearsal so you'd still be able to play baseball."

"Uh … yeah right, but I just don't think—"

This time it's Mia who interrupts. "Coward. That's what you are Dominic Cantrell, a coward."

Then Farhad chimes in. "Which is what you'd expect from somebody who came out of an egg. The guy's a chicken."

I'm still wondering how he knows about that moment in my life. I glance over at Miss Kerver who clearly has no idea what Farhad is talking about. Mia looks grumpy. Foster still looks bored.

David A. Poulsen

"I ... I have to go." I start toward the steps leading down off the stage and to the door. I want out of there. "I've got homework. I'm sorry, Miss Kerver, I really am. I just can't do this."

As I walk out the door, I'm feeling this enormous sense of relief. *Safe at last.*

Which is why I'm not sure how it comes about that one week later I'm on that same stage at noon trying to eat my lunch and be Carlino at the same time.

4

MARCH 8

The Girl in the Window - Part Two

Sometimes I surprise myself.

Now that I was Carlino, I had made up my mind to at least be a good Carlino. Not that I was dumb enough to believe that I actually had any talent as an actor, but I decided I'd at least know my lines and when to come on and off stage—I even learned that stage left kind of feels like stage *right* and vice versa. In case you've never been around a play production, stage left is your left as you are standing on stage looking out at the audience. Which, like I said, feels backward to me but I don't think whoever's in charge of stuff like that is going to change it just because a guy who botched being an egg thinks it's wrong.

Anyway I was pretty busy with rehearsals and schoolwork and I'd started throwing the ball against a

David A. Poulsen

mattress in the basement to get at least a little ready for the coming baseball season. Which brings me to the surprising myself part. It was getting to the time of year when I could spend a little more time on my bike.

I rigged up this sort of mini-music-stand deal that I fastened to my handlebars and I can attach my script to it. That way, as I'm riding around I can "run" my lines (that's another theatre term) and I can glance down if I need to check on a line or a speech. Now I better add here—in case the cops or somebody in authority reads this—that I'm very careful to do this only while I'm stopped or I'm in a back alley or somewhere that I'm not likely to run into something or over someone.

And that's what I'm doing right now—running my lines. I'm getting so I hardly have to look down at my script. That's partly because Carlino doesn't have that many lines—there are three bad guys and I'm definitely the least important of the three plus—spoiler alert—I get killed well before the end of the play.

Anyway, it's a good thing I'm not looking down at my script as I pass the house at 624 Edmund Avenue because I'd have missed her. She's there. She's *there*.

Except this time she's at the front window. The

The Dark Won't Wait

35

house is situated toward the front of the lot which means she's not all that far from me as I ride by. I can see the blue short sleeve top she's wearing. I can see that she's holding a book. And I can also see ... I think ... that she's smiling just like I thought she was the other time. But *is* she smiling at me? Or is she like Mona Lisa, smiling all the time but all mysterious and hard to figure?

Stay cool, Dom, I tell myself. *Stay freaking cool.* I keep going like I've got this really important engagement I have to get to and just barely have time to glance over her way. And a block later I slow down and stop. I have to partly because I realize I've been holding my breath and could keel over any second now. My experience with girls is less than extensive—actually it's close to non-existent. I mean I have girls who are friends, like Mia, but on the romantic side? Not so much. I've had a couple of "sort of" dates that weren't exactly major successes so I'm definitely not in Farhad's league when it comes to knowing the opposite sex. Which might account for my state of mind right now. Which is somewhere between *Huh?* and *Whoa!*

I sit on my bike for a couple of minutes just breathing and thinking. Thinking about a smiling girl who probably wasn't smiling at me. Or maybe it's worse than that. Maybe she's not just smiling; maybe she's actually laughing.

So now I've got a decision to make. Do I ride back the other way—looking all casual—and just happen to glance over that way? Again? Or is that so incredibly obvious that she's going to think I'm the biggest dweeb in the history of dweebdom? And if she wasn't laughing at me before, she will definitely be laughing at me this time. Not *with* me—*at* me.

But I've already made my decision. I've ridden by that house maybe four or five times and this is the only time I've seen her since that first time when I saw her from the McCloy's parking lot. I can't let the opportunity just disappear like air leaving a balloon.

Wait a second. *I've ridden by that house maybe four or five times.* Am I stalking this girl? Am I some creepy guy hoping to … what? … I don't even know what I'm hoping for except maybe to see her. Maybe even talk to her. I haven't followed her. I haven't tried to find her on Facebook. I haven't left weird notes in her mailbox. If this is stalking, then walking across a Starbucks with two cups of coffee and offering one to the girl reading

Chaucer at the corner table—that must be stalking too. At least that's what I'm telling myself as I turn my bike around.

But I don't start right away. I need a plan. If I just ride by she'll think I'm cruising the neighbourhood on my bike which makes me a total loser. Or she'll think I want to meet her but haven't got a clue how. Okay, so what if I stop and wave or maybe I should gesture for her to come outside. But what then? What do I say to her?

Hi there, I was just wondering if your house is for sale. You see, my mom's a realtor and if your parents are thinking of putting ol' 624 on the market we can do a great job for them.

Shut up, Dom! That is the worst idea ever. That's even worse than the fake accident and throwing-myself-to-the-pavement thought that I hate to admit actually passed briefly through my brain on its way to idea purgatory.

So I start riding with no plan—no idea what I'll do when I get to her house.

And there she is ... right there on the front steps. And she *is* smiling. At me. She takes one step down and hesitates, shy maybe, not wanting to look too eager.

I slow down.

David A. Poulsen

"Hi," she says.

"Hi."

I stop and get off my bike, but I don't lay it down. I stand beside it not wanting to move toward her.

"It's nice to meet you," she says.

"Uh, yeah, it's nice to meet you too. I saw you … uh … in the window."

"I know."

"Yeah." *Not really knocking it out of the park on the conversation side, Dom.*

"I figured you must be a nice guy."

"Really? You could tell that from seeing me riding my bike?"

She laughs. It's a soft laugh, a nice laugh. "I saw you with those little kids when you played catch with them. That was cool. No, it wasn't cool. It was just nice."

"Yeah, I guess. I haven't seen you at Hastings."

"We moved into this house after the school year started. I was already enrolled at the Collegiate. My name's Callie by the way."

"Mine's Dom."

There's a silence that lasts just long enough to feel awkward.

Then she says, "So was I right?"

"Right?"

"That you're a nice guy."

"Well, I hope so ... I think so."

"What else?"

"What?"

"What's something else I should know about you?"

For a second I'm stumped by the question. Nobody's ever asked me that before. And because I'm stumped, I say the stupidest thing I've ever said in my life.

"Well, I'm an actor. I'm in the school play this year."

As the words leave my mouth—and can't be taken back—I want to ride my bike over a cliff but as there are no nearby cliffs, instead I make matters worse.

"Baseball," I say.

"The play's called *Baseball*?"

I shake my head.

"It's *about* baseball."

I shake my head again. "No, I mean I'm not really an actor. I mean I'm in a play at school but I'm more of a—"

A voice from inside the house yells, "Callie," and I watch her freeze in place. The smile disappears and she turns and almost runs back toward the house. She stops

David A. Poulsen

at the top of the stairs and turns, says, "Bye," and is gone before I can even answer.

I stay where I am for a couple of minutes thinking ... hoping ... she might come back. She doesn't, so I finally climb back on my bike and head off.

Still cursing myself for telling a girl I really wanted to impress that the thing she should know about me is that I'm an actor, I force my legs to pedal. Still there were a couple of good things. First of all, she thinks I'm a nice guy. And she talked to me and maybe would have talked some more if the person inside the house hadn't called her. I think about that part. It was a man's voice— an unpleasant voice. Her dad maybe, hard to say.

The other good thing is I now have a name—Callie. I kind of like the name. And seeing her up close pretty well confirmed that we're about the same age—also good. I ride off but I'm doing a lot of looking back over my shoulder at 624 Edmond Avenue.

5

MARCH 9

Murder

Mom isn't usually talkative in the morning but today she's full of questions and requests for information. All of it is about the play and I finally push my combo-bowl of corn flakes and fruit loops to one side and decide to give her my full attention.

"I googled it last night," she says. "It sounds interesting ... and kind of scary."

"You're right about that part," I said. "Stephen King called it the scariest movie ever made. And he knows a thing or two about scary. And it's not even a horror flic."

"I read that Audrey Hepburn starred in the movie," Mom says between sips of coffee. "I'm surprised I never saw it. I loved her when I was younger. And she plays a blind woman. I bet she was wonderful in it."

"It was originally a play but it's more famous for the movie. And yeah, Audrey Hepburn played Suzy."

"Maybe we should watch it one night."

I shake my head. "I thought about that but I'm worried that I'd just try to be like the guy in the movie who played my part. Maybe we can watch it after we're done with the play."

"Fair enough as long as it's not too scary. I'm still trying to get over *The Exorcist*."

"Like I said, it's not horror." I don't tell her that *The Exorcist* scared the crap out of me too. "I can give you the main points of the story if you want."

She glances at her watch. "Okay but you've got sixty seconds which means you don't give me every detail of every scene."

Which I admit I have done a few times.

"Okay, so there are three con men, a guy named Roat and his two sidekicks Mike Talman and Carlino, that's me. The bad guys are trying to recover a doll that happens to be full of heroin that was given to Suzy's husband, Sam, at the Montreal airport by a woman named Lisa. Sam doesn't know about the drugs but when Lisa—who is in cahoots with Roat—comes to pick up the doll at Sam and

Suzy's apartment in New York City, Sam can't find it. Roat is a pretty nasty dude; he murders Lisa and sets up a con with Mike and Carlino to get the doll back from Suzy, telling her that the police think Sam is involved in some drug smuggling deal and they need the doll to clear him. Suzy believes that the doll is the key to establishing Sam's innocence but even though she knows where it is, she refuses to give it up. Roat—remember I said he's pretty much pure evil—eventually kills both Mike and Carlino and then it's just this ruthless killer and the blind lady alone in the apartment in a death match."

Mom looks at her watch again. "Nicely done—fifty-five seconds. Kidding aside, I'm glad you're doing this. It's good to try new things. Are you enjoying it?"

I shrug. "I think so ..."

Rehearsals have been okay so far. One of the things Miss Kerver, she's our director, has done—she's cast a girl as Roat. Not a girl dressed up like a guy but Miss Kerver has changed the role of the evil killer to a woman. I don't think she had a choice; there just weren't a lot of guys wanting to be in the play. But the weird thing is that the girl who's Roat, her name is Taylor Melvin—she's amazing as Ms. Roat. Taylor's not very big and

David A. Poulsen

she's really pretty but when she walks on that stage as the villain of the play she is totally a different person. She's badass. She *is* the villain.

"Sounds cool. Can't wait to see it," Mom says. "But you've now gone over your sixty seconds. And I have to go. I'm showing a condo this morning." She takes a last swallow of coffee, kissing me on the ear as she heads for the door. "See you after school. Have a special day."

———————————

Mom nailed it. School the day after my encounter with Callie is better than special. Mostly because I'm pretty sure that the girl I really want to get to know wants to get to know me too.

That and I ace a math quiz—sure it was a small one, not worth a lot as far as my final mark is concerned but still good. During the lunch-hour rehearsal, we block this scene where Carlino and the other two bad guys, Roat and Mike Talman, are in the apartment with Suzy. She can't see us, of course, but she senses something's wrong, that maybe somebody's there. It's a pretty spooky scene and I think it will work really well. Blocking, by the way, is when the actors learn the moves they are supposed to make during each scene in the play. I guess it makes sense. A play isn't just a bunch of people talking on stage—they're actually moving too and every one of those moves is choreographed by the director. I've never thought about that when I've watched plays. That bit where the actor crosses the stage and pours a glass of wine and hands it to the lady wearing the white dress—the actor didn't just think, *Oh, I think I'll wander over and get some wine for Alice there*—no it's all mapped out and timed out. That's blocking.

It isn't until after rehearsal that things get weird—no, weird is definitely not the right word, but I'm not sure what word is the right one.

Mia and Farhad want to go for coffee and there's a Starbucks not too far from school so we head over there for Caramel Fraps, the one thing in this world that all three of us agree on.

It's my turn to buy, which might have a lot to do with how eager they both are to go for coffee, but because I'm still in a really good mood, I'm happy to buy their drinks, and even deliver them while they sit looking at their phones and texting.

Once the drinks are in place and everybody has had one really large gulp and Farhad is over the brain freeze he gets just about every time we have fraps, that's when Mia hits me with the news.

She holds up her phone for me to see. "How weird is that?" she says (there's that word—the *wrong* word—again). "There was a murder right near here."

Since I can't actually see whatever is on her phone, I just shrug and take another sip of the frap—a small sip which is how you avoid the brain freeze, a strategy I've shared several times with Farhad, but he doesn't listen.

"Over on Edmund Avenue."

That's when I sit up and lean over to get a better look at her phone. "Let me see that." I practically yank it out of her hand.

Mia's on the *Daily Herald* site. There's a photograph and the story below it. The photo could have been taken from where I was sitting on my bicycle in front of Callie's house. The thing is, it *is* Callie's house.

"Excuse me," Mia says and holds out her hand for her phone.

"Yeah, just a sec." I lean back and read the story as fast as I can. There's not much detail—no names of victim or suspects—just "the police have nothing further to say except that the investigation continues."

And for the next several minutes it's all I can do to keep breathing and not scream. I can feel Mia and Farhad looking at me but no one says anything. Finally I look away from the phone and up at them.

"I know someone who lives in that house." My voice isn't much more than a whisper.

"Are you serious?' Mia leans forward to look at the screen again.

I nod my head. "Yeah. I mean I don't know her really well or anything but I just saw her there yesterday. Her name's Callie. She's about our age."

"Holy crap, that's crazy." Farhad stops rubbing his head and leans forward. "Was it her that got ... you know ...?"

I shake my head. "It doesn't say." I hold Mia's phone closer and read the story again, this time out loud. "Neighbours reported hearing sounds of a dispute last night, between nine and ten PM, and when police arrived at the scene they found one person deceased. The name of the deceased is not being released until next of kin have been notified and further investigation

David A. Poulsen

takes place." I look up at them and suddenly I'm shaking and I can't stop.

Mia puts an arm around my shoulder. "Hey, take it easy, okay? We don't know if the victim is Callie. Why would somebody murder a kid?"

Victim. I suddenly hate that word. "Are you kidding? There have been lots of kids murdered over the years."

"Well, yeah but—"

"And kids who have committed murders too." Farhad says it in a whisper.

"What are you saying? Are you saying Callie is a—"

"No, no, man, no. That's not what I was saying. I just meant ..." He stops then and a few seconds pass. "What do you think we should do?"

"I don't know." I'm still shaking but it's starting to ease up a little. "I mean it happened last night sometime after I saw her, talked to her. That's so totally unbelievable ..." I don't know how to finish the sentence.

Mia reaches out and takes her phone back. "When your mom picks us up, maybe we could just casually ask her if she could drive by there. We can at least see ... um ... well, I don't know what we'll see. I've never been near a place where a murder's happened except on TV."

"Yeah." I'm nodding like crazy. "That's a good idea. Maybe we can find out a little more. I mean, maybe ..." I stop, because I don't want to finish the thought.

"I know," Mia pats my shoulder. "Maybe we can find out if Callie's okay."

I nod and look at Farhad. He pats my other shoulder. "I'm pretty sure she's okay," he says. "I have a feeling."

Farhad has a lot of feelings. I hope this one is bang on.

We don't talk a lot after that and it's about twenty minutes later that my mom pulls up in front of the Starbucks and comes inside. "You were supposed to text me. It's a good thing I guessed you were here."

"Sorry, I forgot. We got ... doing something and I—"

"Did you hear about the murder? Right in our neighbourhood."

"Yeah, we know about it," I say. "Over on Edmund Avenue. We were thinking—"

"Maybe we should drive by," Mom says. "I've never been anywhere near a murder scene."

Like it's a community event—like seeing the lights at Christmas. Still I want to go by there too.

"Uh ... yeah, sure, that would be okay, I guess."

"I mean I don't want to be all ghoulish or anything."

Mia says, "I'm sure one quick look should be okay."

Mom orders a caramel macchiato and when her drink arrives, we pile into the Satan Wagon. It's probably the quietest the three of us have ever been during the ride home. I'm in the front with Mom, and Mia and Farhad are in the back seat. Farhad seldom goes more than a block or two without making some kind of smart remark but even he seems to understand that murder isn't something you joke about, especially when one of us knows someone who might be involved.

My head is spinning as we get closer to Edmund Avenue. I keep going back to the evening before when I saw Callie and then her father or someone called her back into the house. What was the look on her face? Was it fear or was it just, *Sorry I can't talk to you right now*? What if Callie was the victim? Or what if she was the murderer? Both scenarios seem impossible and yet there was a murder in the house where she's living or staying. The man who called her back inside sounded angry and maybe more than a little mean.

I wonder what we'll see as we drive by 624. I don't

have to wait long to find out. Mom slows down, partly because she has to. Apparently we aren't the only ones wanting to satisfy our curiosity. There's a lineup of cars, gawkers, all moving slowly. And we are about to join the group. A cop is actually directing traffic, or at least keeping it moving, on Edmund Avenue, normally a quiet residential street. The house is on our right. Three police cruisers are parked at the scene, two in the driveway and one on the street. Yellow police tape is set up around the whole yard.

"Holy crap," Farhad says. "It's like one of those CSI shows."

"There was a *murder*, Farhad," Mia says. "What would you expect?"

I roll the window down on my side, hoping to hear something, see something that will at least tell me if Callie is okay.

But the only sound I hear is the cop who's directing traffic. "Keep it moving, folks. C'mon, let's move it along."

As we get alongside the cop, a guy in uniform, not a detective, I tell Mom to stop.

"I can't, Dom, the officer is waving us through."

"Just for a second." I lean my head out the window.

"Sir, I know you're not allowed to say much, but the girl who lives here is a friend of mine and I want to make sure she's okay. Can you just tell me that much?"

"Sorry, kid." He's shaking his head. "You were right the first time. Keep it moving, lady."

I nod and slump back against my seat. "Thanks anyway." I don't know if he hears me.

Mom does as she's told and edges forward, the traffic starting to move a little faster as we get past the house.

"Hey kid."

I sit up and look back at the cop who is looking in our direction. He had to be calling me. I lean my head out the window and he gives me a thumbs-up and a flicker of a smile.

"Thank you," I yell back to him. And roll the window back up. I'm aware that Mom is looking at me.

"I didn't know you knew someone who lives here."

I nod. "Yeah. I mean I don't know her well. Actually not very well at all but ..."

"He's in *looove* with her," Farhad says, then follows it up with a cackle. I knew he couldn't go very long without saying something dumb. Which I guess is okay now that we know Callie isn't the victim.

"Not true," I tell Mom. "I've only seen her a couple of times and talked to her exactly once."

"Okay," Mom says. "How about pizza? We need something to get murder out of our heads or none of us is going to get any sleep tonight." She turns her head partly toward the back seat. "You two text your parents, see if it's okay."

And twenty minutes later we're sitting at Vinnie's Pizza Hideout. The servers all wear these cheesy vests and hats that are supposed to give them the gangster look and the pizzas all have gangster names, like their all-dressed is called "The Mob." Sort of hokey but the pizza's amazing and besides, Mom has a coupon so Vinnie's it is. And at least on this day, the goofy get-ups are kind of appropriate in a creepy sort of way.

Mom says, "I don't know if this was the best choice tonight. If we're trying to get our minds off crime scenes and killers and—"

"It's okay, Mrs. Cantrell," Mia says. "I'm pretty sure we'll all sleep tonight."

"Okay," Mom nods, "but let's not talk about the murder anymore today. How's the play going?"

And that launches Mia and Farhad into a long

discussion about the play, the movie, blindness and Audrey Hepburn. I don't contribute a whole lot to any of it. It's fine for Mom to announce that murder talk is off limits but that doesn't stop me from thinking about it.

6

MARCH 10

Understudy

Mia was wrong about the sleep thing. Turns out I don't get a whole lot of that.

It's 6 AM. I'm still tossing and turning and wrestling with the bed covers. Even though the cop let me know that Callie's okay, I want to know more. I *need* to know more. So at 6:16, I'm in jeans, sweater, Hastings baseball jacket (we won the city championship last year), and my Steph Curry shoes and I'm pedalling for Edmund Avenue.

There's not much traffic so just after 6:35 I'm on Edmund Avenue about five houses away from 624. I know the whole thing is stupid. It's not like Callie's going to be there on the front porch smiling at me like nothing has happened. But when you haven't had much more than maybe an hour's sleep, your brain is a little fuzzy and what seemed like a good idea when you were sneaking out of the house is actually just a giant dork-move a half-hour later.

There's still one patrol car in the driveway; the police tape still has the house and yard barricaded; and one light is on in the kitchen. I picture a couple of officers sitting at the kitchen table drinking cold Timmy's.

I sit on my bike staring at the house for a while and finally decide to pull out my phone and snap a few pictures. I ride past the house, first one way, then the other, grabbing different views of the house. Take away the cop car and the police tape and it could be any house. Except I know that one day ago someone was killed in there.

Murdered in there.

———————————

I'm next to useless at rehearsal. Mia and I are rehearsing a scene where Carlino is pretending to be a cop and questions Suzy about the missing doll. I forget most of the blocking for the scene and wander around like a punch-drunk boxer trying to figure out where I am and why I'm there.

Mia is getting madder as the rehearsal goes on and I'm trying, I really am, but my head is somewhere else.

Miss Kerver finally gives up and ends the rehearsal early. "You two might as well eat your lunch and we'll have another go at this tomorrow." Then she speaks directly to me. "We're getting way too close to opening night for us to have very many rehearsals like this, Dom. Tomorrow I need you to be prepared and familiar with the scene."

"Sorry, Miss Kerver," I mutter. "I know I sucked today. I'll be better tomorrow."

She smiles. "Hey, we all have bad days. Let's just not have too many in a row, okay?"

"Got it." I return her smile and she heads off stage and out of the theatre.

Mia is glaring at me. She is apparently less willing to let me off the hook. "You're not kidding you sucked today. What *was* that?"

"Hey, I was just having trouble getting into it today. Like I told Miss Kerver, I'll be better tomorrow."

"You know what happens in thirty-four days? That's

when we walk out on this stage and there are people in all those seats. *Thirty-four days.*"

"Message received, okay? Seriously, I'll be fine. I'll be more than fine. I will be the next Laurence Olivia."

"It's Laurence Olivi-*er*. You know—"a" as in play—the one we perform in thirty-four days."

I'm thinking she's never going to get off my case. But suddenly she starts laughing. "Did you really just say Lawrence Olivia?"

"Potato, po-taw-to." But now I'm laughing too and the crisis is over. For now. This is the first time I've laughed since I heard about the murder.

But Mia's right. I have to push whatever happened at 624 Edmund Avenue to the back of my mind and concentrate on nailing Carlino. But it would be so much easier if I could see Callie. Talk to her.

The next day I'm better but there's bad news—at least I think it's bad news. Miss Kerver says the show is already almost sold out. That's not the bad news—no the bad news is she's worried that if one of us gets sick it would mean we'd have to cancel a performance or maybe the whole show and refund the money. So she's decided we need to have understudies—that's people who step in and perform a role if an actor gets sick or is arrested or run over by a bus or something. Which would be fine if there were a lineup of kids just dying to make their debut in *Wait Until Dark*. But as you will recall it was all Miss Kerver could do to fill all the roles in the first place, at least the male roles.

So here's the deal. I am understudying Taylor Melvin who is playing Roat, the really evil creep. Like I don't have enough just trying to get Carlino figured out. But maybe what's worse is that Farhad is the understudy for Carlino. (Don't ask me who will be looking after lights and sound while he's on stage.) But get this. Now the guy wants to talk acting all the time. When we're having a coffee or a pop somewhere, he keeps asking me questions about how I think he should stand in this scene or walk in that scene. The man is driving me nuts.

The good news is that Taylor is a health freak—she actually eats fruit and vegetables the way you're supposed to and she's a pretty good athlete so if there's anybody who *shouldn't* get sick, it's Taylor Melvin. Still it means I've got more lines to learn and I need to have at least a rough idea of where Roat is supposed to be on stage, so I really have to pay attention even in the scenes I'm not in. I know it sounds weird that a guy is understudy for a girl but remember Roat in the original play was a guy so I guess it makes sense. Besides, as I said, Ms. Kerver probably didn't have much choice— there weren't many options—or other actors—out there. Anyway, people are just people so maybe it doesn't matter. Maybe anybody can play anybody.

I walk through Roat's stuff a couple of times over the next few days but the only scene of Taylor's (Roat's) I actually have to rehearse is the coolest scene in the play. It happens right after Roat kills Carlino (offstage) and Mike (onstage) and now Roat is in the apartment alone with Suzy. The whole play has been leading up to this moment. Suzy, who is brave and has been outsmarting the bad guys up to now, has run out of time and luck. Her blindness has finally caught up to her and both she and Roat know it. Roat wants the doll and it's pretty obvious to everyone that the minute she gets it, she'll off Suzy and be gone with the drugs. But Suzy isn't about to give up without a fight. She rushes around the apartment with a broom breaking every light in an attempt to even the playing field. If neither of them can see, she at least has a chance because she knows the layout of the apartment and Roat doesn't. But even that stroke of genius, while it buys her a little time, is eventually overcome by Roat. Suzy forgets the light in the refrigerator and Roat opens the door, jams a towel there to hold it open and finally overpowers Suzy.

Except that Suzy has a knife stashed and stabs Roat. But even with that, Roat isn't done. She makes one last effort. Using the knife, she pulls herself along the floor toward Suzy whose last hope is to try to pull the plug on the fridge. As she desperately tries to do that, Roat is able to rise up and throw herself at Suzy, knife raised and ready. At just that moment Suzy pulls the plug, there's a scream and the light goes out and the fridge stops humming. The stage is in total darkness and total silence. The audience doesn't know if Suzy is alive or dead.

A few seconds later the cops arrive, flashlights in hand, with Suzy's husband and the girl who lives next door. They find Roat's body, grotesquely positioned so that it's keeping the fridge door open. They continue to look for Suzy. Finally as one of the officers pulls Roat's body away from the fridge, the door begins to close and there is Suzy, huddled on the floor ... alive.

How cool is that? But even though it's the most amazing scene in the play, and to tell the truth, I didn't think I was that bad when I was Roat in rehearsal ... I'm very glad that Taylor Melvin is playing the part. And still looks healthy. I offered to buy her some of those vitamins you get at the drugstore but I'm pretty sure she thought I was kidding.

I wasn't.

7

APRIL 1

April Fools

It's April 1st.

We've been rehearsing for five weeks and we open in twelve days. And the closer we get to opening night the more I realize that there are a lot of people who would be so much better than me at playing Carlino. Almost everybody. I'm sure nobody in the audience is going to be thinking, *Wow, that guy playing Carlino is hitting a home run.* But Miss Kerver is patient and Mia can't really say anything since it was her badgering that had a lot to do with my finally agreeing to do the stupid play. And besides, ever since our blow-up the day after the murder, I've been busting my backside. Problem is, even though I know my lines and my moves, I don't feel like an actor.

I've ridden past the house at 624 Edmund Avenue a few more times since the murder and not a lot has changed. Except that the police tape has been taken down and there aren't cops around the place. I did find out the name of the victim. I don't know if that means the investigation is over or just that the police are finished with the house part of their work. According to the story in the newspaper, the victim was Shane Krebs, a twenty-four-year-old white male who was originally from the Maritimes and had been in the city only ten months prior to becoming the city's ninth murder victim of the year. As far as I know, no one has been arrested and there has been very little information beyond the name of the deceased man released to the public.

There haven't been any signs of life around 624 Edmund Avenue meaning that whoever was living there at the time of the murder has either moved away, is running from the cops or is waiting a reasonable amount of time before moving back into the house.

And still no word on Callie. Trying to find someone when all you have is a first name and an address that might not even be where she lived is next to impossible and I guess I've sort of given up. But it doesn't stop me from regularly riding by the house on Edmund and looking around the mall on a Saturday afternoon just in case she's having an Orange Julius in the food court or checking out the sweaters at one of the clothing stores.

———————————

Mom, who I don't really think of as a jokester, gets me on April 1 and I have to admit, it's pretty good, but at the same time heartbreaking. Or at least that's what I thought.

Last night (March 31) she got home late so I was already in bed. When I wake up this morning I spend ten minutes or so staring at the cracks in my bedroom's ceiling plaster. It's Friday and it's a teachers' professional development day meaning no school for the students, although we have a run-through of the play later this afternoon. I'm starting to lose interest in the ceiling patterns when I hear a horn honking outside. I ignore it at first but the honking goes on and on. Eventually it starts to bug me so I crawl out from under the covers and stumble my way through the debris on my bedroom floor—books, clothes, baseball cleats, *Wait Until Dark* script, last year's school yearbook and a chocolate chip cookie. I reach down and grab the cookie on my way to the window, thinking it can't have been lying there all that long. Shouldn't kill me.

But it doesn't get eaten.

That's because when I get to the window—my bedroom is on the second floor—I'm looking down at something I thought I'd never see. Mom is standing in the driveway and waving up at me. She's standing next to a Lexus—a *Lexus* for God's sake.

I'm into sweats and a Yankees T-shirt in seconds, down the stairs two at a time, past the kitchen that's sending out a spectacular blend of smells—pancakes and bacon cooking. I figure it's got to be a celebration breakfast now that we're Lexus owners. At the front door I pull on my Under Armour Curry 3's—no socks, no time—and I'm out the door.

There's a skiff of snow on the front lawn and it's pretty cold but I barely notice that as I get to the car in maybe four strides.

"Wow, this is amazing, Mom!" I realize I'm shouting but hey this is big.

"I was pretty sure you'd think it's a pretty cool car." She grins at me. "Of course, it's not new."

"Of course not. Who cares?" I run my hands over the front fender. "What did they give you for the Satan Wagon?"

She doesn't answer that. She's got her phone out and I figure she wants us to grab a couple of selfies—part of the celebration. I open the passenger-side door and look inside. There's some stuff on the back seat—odd but I figure it's probably stuff that was in the Satan wagon. I close the door and straighten up.

"Wow," I say again. "It kind of looks like Barstads' but nicer, of course." The Barstads live one block over—their daughter Julie is in a couple of my classes and Mom is pretty good friends with her mom—I think her name is Ellen.

"It does look like Barstads', doesn't it?"

I haven't stopped looking at the car but I look at Mom now. She's holding out her phone showing me something. *What's happening here?* Then, as I look at the phone I realize exactly what has happened. Mom's phone is on her calendar. The date is April 1.

"Oh no," I whisper. "This *is* Barstads' car isn't it?"

"Uh-huh."

"And this is April Fool's."

"Uh-huh."

"Aaagh." I'm pretty sure they can hear my anguish at Barstads' house. I start a slow walk back to the house, contemplating the various methods of self-destruction.

"Dom?"

I stop and turn back to her.

"Do you remember last year? When I swore revenge?"

I nod. "I remember but the fake rat in your underwear drawer is nowhere near as cruel as making me think that the days of the Satan Wagon were over."

"Oh, I don't know. That was as close as I've ever been to a heart attack—I call that fairly cruel."

I shrug. "Yeah, I guess so. Anyway you got me. We're even."

"Not quite." She's enjoying this way too much.

"Are you kidding me? This is a dagger to my very heart; this is lower than low; this is cruel and heartless; this is a whole herd of rats in the underwear drawer ... this is—"

"Shut up for a minute." She holds up her hand. "Even with all your drama, you've missed what this really is. This is one of the greatest April Fool's pranks of all time because it's actually a *double* prank."

"A double prank? What does that even mean?"

"It means don't ever mess with your mother is what it means."

I don't have an answer for that so I just stare at her wondering if Mom downed a couple of glasses of wine while she was getting the pancakes and bacon going.

"Because, you see, you thought this was our car, then you realized you were wrong, that it isn't our car but actually you were wrong again because it actually *is* our new car. I bought it from the Barstads—so that makes it a double prank."

She's grinning again but now I don't know whether to believe her or not. I mean what if it's a triple prank and I get all excited again and she says, *Ha, gotcha again!* The woman's diabolical.

"Oh, and one more thing. They didn't really want the station wagon as a trade in so we still own it. You're a month from getting your license and when that happens that will be your car."

"Seriously?"

"Actually I am totally serious. The Lexus isn't all that new—it's a 2017—but it's what we can afford and it's a whole lot newer than the station wagon and the

Barstads have kept it in really good shape. So I guess we're a two-car family now."

Right on cue, Ellen Barstad pulls up to the curb in front of the house. She's at the wheel of the Satan Wagon and the atmosphere is suddenly changed. A blue cloud billows out behind the fake wood rear door accompanied by the noise that I realize is a lot louder than when you're inside the car.

But none of that matters. Not anymore. Because this is no longer just that god-awful car. It's *my* god-awful car. And as cool as the Lexus is, it's got nothing on my car—my Satan Wagon.

Mrs. Barstad climbs out of the car and she and Mom talk and giggle for a while. I realize that this is one of those stories that will be told at family dinners for decades. And I have to realize Mom's right. She got me. Twice.

As Mrs. Barstad waves and heads off down the block toward her house, Mom throws an arm around my shoulder and musses my hair with her other hand.

"You know something?"

She looks at me still smiling. "What?"

"Dad would have loved this."

We don't talk about Dad much but I think about

him a lot and I know Mom does too. He loved to laugh and to make other people laugh.

"You're right. He would have."

We both stand there for a minute, both of us smiling, remembering. And it's nice.

Mom's the one to finally speak. "Let's go have some pancakes—I've got a feeling they're going to taste really good this morning."

"As long as they're *real* pancakes."

We both laugh at that and head for the house.

8

APRIL 13

Drama

For the next twelve days my life is the play. Luckily, school isn't too bad during that twelve days, no exams, not even from Ms. Faver who's my social teacher and likes to throw quizzes at you like Gerritt Cole fastballs.

I haven't really minded being in the play except for the fact that Foster MacLennan has turned out to be pretty much a jerk. He barely talks to me except when we're on stage and he's often just totally rude. No rude is *not* the right word at all. Like Tuesday, two days before opening, Farhad sat in on the noon rehearsal which was running lines. Miss Kerver had to be at a staff meeting so it was just the actors and Farhad. We weren't on stage; we were just sitting around saying our lines and eating our lunch. Farhad was the only one with a script and he was cueing us if we forgot a line. At one point he'd just taken a giant bite of sandwich and Foster forgot his line. We had to wait while Farhad chewed as fast as he could so he could actually talk.

After a few seconds of waiting—ten or fifteen seconds at the most—Foster said, "Come on, Brownie, if you're going to be a prompter, you need to actually prompt."

Silence. Total silence.

I couldn't believe what I'd just heard but before I could say anything, Foster laughed and said, "Okay, I can see by the looks on everybody's faces we're a politically correct cast here so I apologize. Just take your time, Farhad; cue me when you get around to it."

It was a pretty uncomfortable moment, especially for Mia who I'm pretty sure thinks Foster is kind of special. Farhad got up and left but no more was said and we ran lines for another fifteen minutes or so; then everybody headed off to class.

I texted Farhad after the rehearsal ended to tell him I thought Foster's comment was a total jerk move. He texted me back to say he was used to it from creeps like that. *Used to it?* Like that stuff happens a lot? And if it does, why hasn't Farhad told me about it before this?

My first class after lunch was math but I didn't spend much time thinking about math.

———————————

It's opening night. Mia, who has been in lots of plays, has tried to let me know what this night would be like. And I have to admit she was pretty close. But even with her coaching, when it actually arrives, I'm terrified. In fact, if I had my license, I might make a run for it in the Satin Wagon (yeah, that's the new name—*Satin* because that baby is *so* smooth).

Everybody is nervous, even Rebecca (don't call me Becky) Rashad, a Grade 9 student who is President of the Drama Club and is one of the makeup people. We had makeup for our dress rehearsal and she was fine, but tonight she keeps making mistakes and is constantly rubbing off whatever she's done to my face and re-doing it. And talking. I'd like to be just sitting here thinking about my lines but she hasn't stopped talking since she started applying my base.

Some people, like Mia, do their own makeup, but I tried it and I looked stupid, so I'm leaving it in the hands of Rebecca. Which means I now know everything there is to know about her older sister, Rana, and her baby sister, Sylvan, and I also know Rebecca's opinions on everything in the world—Drake, Facebook, Nickelback and Taylor Swift—*she loves* them—chemistry, socks with sandals, red meat and Kanye West—*meh.*

Did I mention that terror has set in? For me at least. Not nervousness, not stage fright, I'm talking about total, all-in terror.

And now it's time. Rebecca gives me one last critical look and nods. "Perfect," she says, "Break a leg." Which, of course is what theatre people say to each other. You never say g_ _d l_ _k to an actor because exactly the opposite is apparently what will happen. So break a leg it is. Unless you are Farhad Shirvani, Mr. Comedy. He poked his head in the dressing room a few minutes ago and called, "Break a leg, everybody; break an egg, Dom." Ha ha.

Our stage manager calls, "Places, beginners, please!" And we move to the backstage areas we will make our entrances from. A minute later I'm standing in the wings. The lights go down and this cool suspenseful music Farhad found somewhere begins. There's no turning back. The lights come up and Foster MacLennan (Mike) knocks on the door to Suzy's apartment; he knocks twice, then opens the door and lets himself into the apartment. From where I am, I can see him moving around the apartment checking closets, looking in the bathroom, opening then closing the drapes. My cue.

———————————

And suddenly, I swear to God, I can't remember my first line. Which is ridiculous ... my first line is "You!" Suddenly my mind takes me back to my last time on a stage ... the egg disaster. I shrug that off, take a deep breath, step to the apartment door and ring the bell. Here we go.

———————————

The first act is over. Rebecca is touching up my makeup but for once she's not talking. That's because Ms. Kerver is talking. To be honest, she sounds more like a football or hockey coach than a director. It's all, *You guys were awesome in the first act; you just have to keep it up in the second act, and we can do this thing like it's never been done.* Then she goes around the room patting everybody on the shoulder like we're offensive linemen. I wonder for a minute if she's about to lead us in one of those *ooh-ooh-ooh—who's got heart/we've got heart—who's got guts/we've got guts* kind of pregame yells before we head back on stage. Thankfully she stops short of that.

I mean I can understand her excitement. She's been working on this for pretty much the whole school year—it's a big deal and I think we actually surprised her in that first act. Everybody's feeling good as we take our places for Act Two.

The best part is that my place for the start of Act Two is in the dressing room. I'm not on for a while so I sit and run my lines with Rebecca helping me—giving me my cues. She's kind of cooled all the Drake and Swifty chatter and is actually helpful. And then just out of the blue she says, "You know you're really good at this. You're an amazing Carlino." Which changes my opinion of her from that pain-in-the-butt niner to that talented, funny and actually sort of cute makeup person.

———————————

I'm only in one scene in the second act, then I get killed, which means I can race around to the back of the house (auditorium doors) and watch the final scene with Roat and Suzy. My stuff goes okay and the final scene is amazing. Just about everybody in the audience jumps and gasps when Roat dives across the stage and grabs Suzie. In fact, that last scene is so good, I'm still standing at the back of the theatre as the play ends. Now if you know anything about plays you know that the cast comes onstage at the end to take a bow. Except I'm still in the auditorium applauding my fellow actors and I have totally forgotten about the bow. Which, by the way, we rehearsed several times.

"Damn!" I yell it pretty loud but luckily the audience is applauding like crazy so I don't think anybody hears me. And I run. Now one thing I can do pretty well is run. I led our baseball team in stolen bases last year and that's about how fast I'm going as I race for backstage. I get there just as everybody is walking back out on stage. Now I don't know if I should go out on stage or just forget it. Ms. Kerver sees me and practically screams, "Go, go, go!" So I do and make a sliding stop next to Mia just as everybody begins their bow. I bow. And I'm pretty sure I can hear some chuckling in the audience. And I *know* I can hear Mia say, "Once an egg always an egg." But as we straighten up I can see she's smiling. The audience is getting louder and Mia and Taylor Melvin step forward and take a bow, then turn to Foster MacLennan and me. We move up alongside them for a final bow.

I finally look out at the audience and everybody in that auditorium is standing and clapping and some are even whistling. It's pretty cool. Mia turns her head slightly to me and says, "We killed it."

"Yeah we did," I say.

———————————

And that's it. The curtain finally closes and all of us, the cast and crew and even Ms. Kerver are hugging and high-fiving. It's probably ten minutes before we finally leave the stage and head back toward the dressing room.

Except we don't get there because the hallway between the stage and the dressing room is packed with people.

Parents, brothers and sisters, teachers, other students ... it feels like everybody is there and they are all smiling and congratulating us. My mom gives me a couple of near back-breaking hugs. "I am so proud of you," she says, maybe fourteen times. Finally she turns to talk to my math teacher, Mr. Goplen, who is telling her how great "all the kids were."

Somebody touches my arm and I turn expecting to see Farhad or one of the neighbours or a teacher but it isn't any of those people.

It's Callie.

And for the second time that night, I completely forget my line. Luckily, she's a lot more together than I am.

"Hi," she says. "Congratulations. You were fantastic. Everyone was. And you were right—this is something I should definitely know about you."

I don't get it at first but then I remember that day in front of her house.

"Uh ... yeah, thanks," I stammer. "I ... uh ... didn't know you'd ... I mean ... uh ... I'm glad you came tonight. And I'm glad you liked the play."

"I loved it." She smiles that amazing smile. "Except for that last part. I've never screamed so loud in my life."

"Yeah, it's a pretty cool scene all right."

I laugh. She laughs. And right about there, conversation dries up like a mudhole on the desert. I look at her and she looks at me. I can tell she's about to leave and that is the one thing I do not want to happen.

"Um, how are you anyway, I mean how is everything? I was worried about you when I heard about ..."

She nods her head but the laughter and smile are gone now. Obviously this isn't something she wants to talk about. At least not right here and not right now.

"I hope you're not mad that I mentioned it," I tell her. "I mean it's none of my business. And you don't have to tell me anything. I'm just glad you're all right."

"I'm okay and I'm not mad."

"Great."

I'm starting to realize that this is the most boring, simple-minded conversation in the history of words. I've got to do better. But I may be out of time. She's looking around like she's supposed to meet somebody. But then she surprises me.

"Can you sign my program?" She hands me a pen.

David A. Poulsen

"Sure." I realize this is another part of being an actor I didn't think about. I should have some cool one-liner I use when people want me to sign their program. My mind races and I come up with ... nothing. And that's about what I write.

To Callie. I'm glad you were here tonight and I'm so glad you liked the play. Dom Cantrell.

Could I be more boring? I hand her the program, she reads it and smiles. "That's great," she says.

Which I know is her being polite and probably thinking ... *Hmm, Dom, not that far from dumb.*

"Can I just ask you one thing?" I say.

"Sure."

"What's your last name?"

She gets kind of a funny look on her face. "What would you do if you knew my last name?"

"Well, you know, I could ... uh ... maybe call you ... or something."

She reaches into her purse and pulls out something that looks like a business card. She hands it to me.

I look at it, then at her. "You have business cards?"

She laughs and leans into me and kisses me on the cheek. "Just one," she says, laughing. "You were awesome."

And then she turns and disappears into the crowd. I spend the next minute or so trying to figure out the kiss. Was it a congratulations kiss? An *I'd like to get to know you better kiss*? Or does she give out kisses when she gives out business cards? That thought reminds me that I'm still holding onto it. I look down at the words— they're hand-written in a beautiful handwriting—like that, what's it called ... calligraphy.

Callie Snowden

This card is for the boy on the bicycle

This card is for the boy in the play

This card is for the boy I hope will call me

989-6007

I'm still staring at the card when I hear ...

"Pretty girl."

I turn and see Mom smiling at me like she's a cat with a mouse.

"Yeah, she is."

"Friend from school?"

"No, that's the girl from the house where the murder happened."

Mom's head goes up and she's looking off at the crowd of people, the smile gone.

I watch her for a second. "What?"

She shakes her head. "I ... just ... I wish I'd said something, that's all. That must have been so terrible for her."

"I don't know, Mom. I think she prefers not to talk about it."

"I can understand that. She looks really nice."

"I don't really know her that well yet, but yeah, I think so."

"You know her well enough that she gave you her phone number."

"What? Oh, yeah, it's right here on ... um ... this ... uh ... card here."

"Well, I think that's pretty cool." She's smiling again. "It's been quite a night."

And finally I begin to relax. "Yeah, I guess it has."

"Did I mention I'm really proud of you?"

We both laugh. "Actually, you did." I give her a hug.

"Hey, Mrs. Cantrell." I'm still hugging Mom but I recognize the voice. Farhad.

"Hi, Farhad," Mom gives him a hug too. "The sound and lights were wonderful."

"Thanks, Mrs. Cantrell. It wasn't easy making some of these actors look good but I did what I could."

Mom laughs—she always laughs at Farhad's dopey comments—then Farhad punches me on the arm. "Hey, I need to talk to you, man."

Mom turns to talk to some other parents and Farhad and I move a few steps away.

"Dom, you won't believe it. At least six chicks have been hitting on me already tonight." He's grinning and talking even faster than usual. "This sound and lights gig is awesome. Maybe for next year's play you should try it. You know, I mean it's great visiting with your mom and everything, but, well, you know what I mean ..."

For once Farhad's nonsense doesn't annoy me. "You know, maybe you're right. Maybe if I was a techie guy, girls would pay attention to me, maybe even give me their business card or something."

He shakes his head sadly, like he realizes there's no hope for me. "See, that's what I'm talking about. You don't even know how it works. No chick is going to give you a business card."

"Oh, yeah, you're probably right."

I'm grinning as I slide Callie's card into my pocket and Farhad and I head over to where Ms. Kerver is trying to line everybody up for photos. Facebook here we come.

9

APRIL 17

Disappearance

The last two performances of *Wait Until Dark* went fairly smoothly. We didn't make any major mistakes and the audiences seemed to really enjoy the play. But ... I don't know ... it all seemed like a bit of a letdown after that amazing opening night. I guess that's natural. We could never re-create the excitement all of us felt after that first performance.

And, of course, for me it was special that Callie had been in the audience, had come backstage and had given me a card with her contact info on it. I looked for her on each of the other two nights of the play, but she wasn't in the audience or if she was, she didn't come backstage again.

Which is partly why I'm a lost cause in English. It's

the Monday after Saturday's final performance so you'd think I'd have settled down by now but I won't lie—I haven't. We started the poetry unit today and I'm okay with poetry, at least some of it (even though I can't write any that isn't total crap) but I just can't concentrate. Mostly I'm arguing with myself about how long I should wait before I call Callie. Oh, and there's that whole *What do we talk about and should I ask her out on the first call* internal debate going on as well. So poetry doesn't really have much of a chance, at least not today.

I look over at Mia and she doesn't look like she's really into English today either ... but for a very different reason. Mia is huge after her performance in *Wait Until Dark.* A reporter from the *Daily Herald* was at the performance on Saturday night and interviewed her and took a ton of photos of her as well. The review of the play in this morning's newspaper was mostly about Mia. And with good reason, I guess. She was pretty amazing.

The guy took some shots of the rest of us too and even talked to a couple of the other actors although he apparently didn't think the guy who played Carlino deserved a whole lot of attention. Actually my effort was worth exactly one line in the paper although I

David A. Poulsen

will say the line was okay: *Dominic Cantrell brought an interesting mix of nervous and nasty to the role of the petty criminal, Carlino.* Which isn't all that bad. At least he didn't say I sucked. I'm okay with not getting a lot of love in the *Daily Herald*, given the attention I got from one particular person.

And speaking of attention, Mia is also going to be interviewed on the local TV station, some arts scene show. I have to say Mia's been pretty good about it. I mean she's enjoying the fame, for sure, but she's trying to be the same person she was before she was Suzy the blind lady, and I think she's doing pretty well. Of course if she does get snooty and too big for the rest of us, there's always Farhad who is a master at bringing people back to earth if they start thinking and acting like they're special.

Ms. Lathrop is really into poetry—she's told us it's her favourite part of the course—and I'm feeling bad that I'm pretty much mailing it in. Or at least I was until a couple of minutes ago. Ms. Lathrop is showing us photos she took during her summer vacation in England. The pictures are of this graveyard called Stoke Poges and they're actually kind of cool. And it turns out the graveyard is the setting and part of the inspiration for a poem by a guy named Thomas Gray. It's called "Elegy Written in a Country Churchyard," and with the photos scrolling through on the smart board and the lights out in the classroom, Ms. Lathrop reads the poem to us or at least most of it.

I'm knocked out by it. I guess I'd never really noticed it but Ms. Lathrop has an amazing voice for reading and she makes the poem and all of its images totally come alive—which is probably a really stupid way to describe a poem about death. She finishes reading, then turns off the smart board and turns on the lights and it's weird but I'm disappointed. I wanted the poem to go on for a while longer. It's not exactly cheerful, not with lines like, "Each in his narrow cell forever laid, The rude forefathers of the hamlet sleep." The "narrow cell," if you haven't read the poem, is the grave.

But it's not depressing either. It feels like it's as much about the lives of these people as it is about their being dead.

English is our last class on Mondays and I'm excited to get out of the school and to the bench. I want to see what Mia and Farhad thought of the poem. But when I get there Mia's on her phone and Farhad isn't there. Mia ends her call and she's excited.

"There's this semi-professional drama group and they want me to try out for a part in their next production. How cool is that?"

"Where's Farhad?"

Her face falls and I realize I was totally rude. "Hey, I'm sorry, that *is* cool. But I'm not surprised. The word is out that you were awesome in *Wait Until Dark*. Which you were. Today it's the theatre group in the city. Tomorrow it's Hollywood."

She punches me on the arm, but the smile is back on her face.

"Yeah, right." She tries to look modest but it's not working. "Anyway I haven't seen Farhad since the end of English class. He grabbed his coat out of his locker and raced out the door. I thought he was coming here."

I shrug. "That's weird. Anyway he'll probably be here in a couple of minutes. What did you think of the poem?"

"Well, it was kind of depressing but I thought Ms. Lathrop's photos were great and it kind of rocked to be looking at the actual graves that the guy wrote about like 250 years ago."

"I know and the way the poet, that Thomas Gray guy described—" Her phone rings and she holds up a hand like, *Hold that thought and we'll come back to that when I'm finished talking to my agent.*

She wanders off like suddenly she needs privacy with her calls. So I take out my own phone and text Farhad.

Where are you?

I wait for the ping to tell me he's answered but no ping, no answer. I look around. And no Farhad. That's just strange.

Mia strolls back over to where I'm standing but she's forgotten what we were talking about. Or she just got another acting offer. Anyway, she's smiling one of those smiles that has nothing to do with the person she's smiling at—in this case, me—and everything to do with a call that has made her feel good about herself. I can see she's not about to tell me who it was or what the call was about and I'm okay with that because I'm starting to worry about Farhad. Maybe he got some kind of bad news and he had to be somewhere right away.

Mia has finally noticed something is amiss. "Where's Farhad?"

David A. Poulsen

"Yeah, that's kind of what I was trying to ask *you*. But then Steven Spielberg called and—"

She doesn't miss the sarcasm and she's angry. "I'd have thought my friends would be excited for me."

"One of your friends is excited for you." I soften my voice a bit. "Honestly I am. The problem is the other friend, the one who is always here ... is *not* here."

She looks around like she expects Farhad to be somewhere close by. "Okay, that's kind of wrong. I mean something could have come up, but you'd think he'd have let us know. Did you try texting him?"

"Yeah, thirty seconds ago. Nothing. At least not yet. What do we do if your mom shows up and he still isn't here?"

Right on cue, Mia's mom pulls up in front of the school in a Jeep Grand Cherokee. Black, just one year old, nice ride. She waves at us to come and get in the car; obviously she's in a hurry. Mia and I look at each other and walk over to the car. Mia leans in the passenger side window.

"Hey, Mom."

"Come on guys. Let's go. The decorator is going to be at the house in twenty minutes."

Mia doesn't move. "We've got a bit of a problem. Farhad isn't here."

"I can see that, but actually that's Farhad's problem not ours. Let's go."

I bend down and smile across at Mia's mom. "He shouldn't be very long, Mrs. Stark."

She shakes her head vigorously. "Sorry, Dom, but I have to go now. Jump in and let's roll."

Mia and I straighten up in unison. Her shoulders lift in a *You can't reason with them* shrug.

"You go," I tell her. "I'll stay here. If there's something going on, I better stick around in case he needs help or whatever."

"We both know Farhad needs help." She's trying for a little humour because I think she's embarrassed about her mom being so impatient.

I smile at the joke. "I'll call you later and let you know what's going on."

"Mia." Mrs. Stark actually revs the engine. I want to say *Seriously?* But I figure it might be smarter to keep my mouth shut. Mia gets in the car but sort of takes her time doing it. Making a point. She looks up at me and rolls her eyes and then they're gone.

I walk back toward the school, throw my book bag on the metal bench and sit down. I stare at my phone like giving it a dirty look will get some action. It doesn't work. And to make things a little worse, a cold wind comes up, turning what was a decent weather day into one suddenly a lot less pleasant.

I text Farhad again.

Call me or text me, bro.

But he doesn't and it's weird but I sort of knew he wouldn't. I'm getting a little worried. This isn't Farhad. Something's wrong.

Fifteen minutes drift by at the speed of a wounded worm. And now it's not just cooler, it's cold. I look around. Nobody. The students have all left. Even the teachers' parking lot is almost empty. It's a half-hour walk home and it feels like it could rain or snow or something. I decide to head out. I keep looking around and behind me the whole walk/jog home hoping to see Farhad. I wish he'd suddenly show up all out of breath with some crazy story about what happened to keep him from our regular after-school rendezvous. Farhad being Farhad.

But I don't see him.

Supper, homework, then an hour spent reading the manual for my car. Now there's a couple of words that feel good in my mouth.

My car.

And, yes, Mom somehow found a manual for a 1981 Plymouth Reliant—I think maybe eBay—and presented it to me last night as a surprise present/ reward for my performance in *Wait Until Dark*. I didn't know people got presents for being in plays. There were some bouquets floating around on opening night and we all got posters signed by everybody in the cast and crew but I guess a few people thought surprises at the end of the run would be nice too.

Mia got enough flowers to start a florist shop, Miss Kerver's boyfriend is taking her to New York as soon as school's out to see some plays on Broadway and Foster MacLennan is going spring skiing with his parents. Taylor Melvin's parents took her out to dinner at the healthiest restaurant in town. But nobody is happier than the kid who got the car manual for a forty-two-year-old station wagon.

But as cool as the manual is, I'd be a lot happier if I had some idea what's going on with Farhad. I've texted him three more times and phoned twice. Nothing.

It's nine o'clock and I can't stand it anymore. I decide to ride over to his place on my bike. It's maybe a twenty-minute ride but at least whatever weather system brought the cold air earlier has apparently moved on. It's not summer out there but it's not bad. I alternate my thoughts between Farhad and Callie, both of them somewhat puzzling to me.

When I get there, Farhad's house is in total darkness. Mr. Shirvani's Audi isn't in the driveway. So maybe the family was called away; there's a sick relative or something. But that doesn't explain why Farhad hasn't called me back or replied to any of my texts.

Now I'm really worried about the guy but there's not much more I can do. As I'm riding back home, Mia texts me to ask if I've heard from Farhad. My answer is short.

No, something's wrong. Got to be.

She tells me not to worry, there has to be a reasonable explanation, a line that you hear all the time on cop and medical shows on TV. Trouble is it means nothing. I decide to hit the shower then bed. What I'm hoping

The Dark Won't Wait

is that tomorrow is going to be so ordinary, it will be boring. Boring would be better than sweating what's happened to my best friend.

10

APRIL 18

The Assembly

Yeah, so much for boring.

That goes out the window about three minutes after I arrive at school. Farhad isn't here. Not at the bench, not in the hallway and not at his locker. Not in homeroom. Not at his desk two rows to the right of mine. Nowhere.

More texts. More *unanswered* texts.

But it's during second period that things get really strange. We're about five minutes into social when a weird message comes over the intercom. Mr. Turley, our school principal, isn't a guy who needs to draw attention to himself. So he isn't usually on the intercom. But he is this time. And what he's saying is that a special assembly is happening right now and could teachers please escort their classes to the gym as soon as possible.

Which is why I'm sitting next to Mia looking at the stage where just a few days before we were performing *Wait Until Dark*. And if I didn't know better I'd think the assembly had something to do with the play. That's because on stage with Mr. Turley are two police officers, one man and one woman. Everybody is looking totally serious. I notice there are some adults at the back of the gym leaning against the wall.

Mia turns to me and whispers, "What if this is about Farhad? What if he's ...?"

She doesn't finish the thought but I have a pretty good idea where she was going with it. I don't answer because right then Mr. Turley steps up to the microphone. All the hushed chatter that was going on ends right there. I guess everybody is thinking the same thing I am. *This is serious stuff.* Although I'm praying that it isn't as serious as Mia was about to suggest.

I focus on Mr. Turley. I've always really liked him, I guess partly because he played professional football before he became a teacher. He played three years with the Toronto Argonauts of the CFL. He's a big guy, probably six-two or -three, maybe 220 or 230 pounds and he's African–Canadian with a shaved head.

Every morning he's out in the hall, talking to kids as we arrive for school. I think he knows most of the names of the kids and he knows maybe a thousand jokes and one-liners that he tries out on us as we go past him on the way to our home rooms. Sometimes we roll our eyes if we've heard it before or if it's a really dumb one (quite a few of them are), but I think just about every kid in the school thinks it's cool that the boss of the school is out there wanting to start our day with a smile.

But I'm guessing there won't be any jokes or one-liners right now. Mr. Turley clears his throat and the place gets still quieter.

"Students, teachers, parents. I felt it was best to bring you all together to hear some very unfortunate news. And to provide information that we hope will reduce the *misinformation* that tends be front and centre at times of crisis."

Mia and I look at each other. She mouths the word *crisis* at me and I nod. Not a good sign.

Mr. Turley looks around the auditorium as he continues. "With me on stage today are two members of our police service who will share that news with you. To my immediate right is Constable McCartney and on her right is Staff Sergeant Wheeler. I believe Constable McCartney will speak first."

The female officer steps up to the microphone. She glances down at a small card she is holding, probably with some notes on it, then she looks up at all of us. I'm guessing there are more than a thousand people in the gymnasium right at that moment. And every eye is on that constable.

"Yesterday morning when the father of one of the students here at Hastings Park High School arrived at his place of business—a pharmacy—he discovered that the building had been broken into overnight. Some drugs were taken though that did not appear to be the main motive for the break-in. There was considerable damage done to the premises but most disturbing was the fact that in three different locations inside the pharmacy and at another location on the outside of the building, racist slogans and comments, some threatening in nature, were spray-painted on the walls. I'm not going to detail exactly what was written but the pharmacist is from Pakistan and the comments were crude and derogatory in nature. They were also violent in terms of threatening the pharmacist and his family if they did not get out of our community and go back where they belong." She makes air quotes as she says "back where they belong."

"I'm paraphrasing and clearly not repeating the profanity that was part of the messages, but I hope you are able to get the basic tone and intent from what I have said. I'm going to turn the microphone over to Staff Sergeant Wheeler who has a request for each of you."

She hasn't mentioned any names but I already know who she's talking about. There's only one kid in the school whose dad is from Pakistan and runs a pharmacy. That person is Farhad. Mia and I look at each other again and I can tell she's thinking the same thing I am. We look back to the stage as the female officer steps back and the second police officer steps up to the microphone.

He's about the same size as Mr. Turley but quite a bit younger. "You are probably wondering how this impacts you." He pauses but I already know what's coming next. "As Constable McCartney has told you, the gentleman who owns and operates the pharmacy is the father of one of your fellow students. His name is Jameel Shirvani and his son Farhad attends Hastings. First of all, I want you all to know that everyone in the Shirvani family is okay, including Farhad. As you can imagine, all of them are shaken and, as a matter of fact, so are we. This is not a community where we've encountered a lot of this kind of thing in the past and clearly it's something we want to end as quickly as possible. And most of the time, this is where it ends, with no further violence or cruelty after the perpetrators have passed along their message. But we can't know that for certain.

"We will be doing everything we can to apprehend the perpetrators. While I can't go into details about our investigation I can tell you that we believe the persons who did this are young people. It is possible that someone in this school may know the people involved in the vandalism and theft at Shirvani's Pharmacy. If any one of you has any information or should encounter information in the days ahead that you can share with us, we would very much appreciate your help. Your names will be kept confidential. And if you are reluctant because you feel that you can't rat out another kid or kids, please think about this. We asked your principal to bring you all together so we could speak directly to you, and the reason is this. This is a hate crime. The threats that were part of these messages were both violent and graphic in nature. And we believe they need to be taken seriously. How would you feel if you had information that might assist us in the investigation and you withheld that information and harm came to one or more members of the Shirvani family? None of us wants that. Your teachers will all have a number they will give to you when you get back to your classrooms. Please call with whatever information you might come to possess, no matter how trivial. And one last thing. We do not want any of you to try to play detective or become some sort of vigilantes to try to even the score for your fellow student. If you think you know something that might help us, call the number you'll receive and leave the police work to us. Thank you."

The officer looks around, then steps back as Mr. Turley moves again to the microphone. To be honest I've stopped listening. My body feels completely numb and my mind is racing around and making no sense at all. Mia is staring straight ahead but one large tear is trickling slowly down her cheek. She doesn't move to wipe it away.

Mr. Turley must have dismissed us to return to class as students are all up and moving, some talking, a lot of them silent. I wished the police had allowed us to ask questions but I also realized the ones I wanted to ask were mostly personal, like when is Farhad coming back to school.

"It's somebody in this school." Mostly I'm thinking it but I say it out loud.

"What?"

"You heard the police." I look at Mia. "It's young people. Students. It's people at this school. I've seen them look at Farhad; you can see the hate in their faces."

Mia shakes her head. "First of all, they didn't say the people who broke into Mr. Shirvani's drugstore were students. Not all young people go to school and not all young people in this town go to *this* school. And I've never seen what you're talking about. I'm sure there are people here who don't like Farhad but I don't think it's because of his skin colour or where he comes from."

"What are you talking about?" I realize I'm getting a little louder than I need to be. "If you haven't seen it, you must walk around the halls with your eyes closed. What about Foster?"

"Foster? Foster MacLennan?"

"The 'Brownie' comment. You didn't hear it?"

David A. Poulsen

She thinks about it. "I heard it and I know it was wrong. And I also know Foster feels bad about that."

"Are you talking about that crap apology that wasn't really an apology? Come on, Mia."

"No, I'm not talking about that. I know Foster feels bad about that because he told me he feels bad about it."

I kind of thought there might be something going on between Mia and Foster but I decide this isn't the time to bring that into the conversation.

"Anyway, that's just an example."

The truth is, until this morning's assembly, I probably haven't spent thirty seconds thinking about racism at Hastings High. I'm not sure why. I guess until it smacks you in the face, you don't give it much thought. What I said to Mia about the hate in people's faces when they looked at Farhad, that was BS. If it was there, I didn't see it. Or if I did I ignored it. What does that make me?

I turn to Mia to apologize or at least admit she's right but I don't get the chance.

Mr. Turley is beside us. I didn't notice him coming our way but I notice him now, the same serious look on his face that we saw when he was on stage. "I wonder if you two would mind coming by my office before you head back to class."

Mia says, "Sure," and I nod my head. I guess our faces must be giving us away because Mr. Turley manages a small smile.

"You're not in any trouble and, as the officer said in the assembly, Farhad is okay. I'd just like to chat with you for a minute."

I nod again and Mr. Turley's gone. Several students are looking at us. They're probably thinking the same thing I was when Mr. Turley came up to us ... *Oh, crap, this has to be bad.*

I look at Mia. "I guess he meant now, right?"

"I think so."

We head off in the direction of the office but neither of us is walking very fast. Despite Mr. Turley's assurance that we aren't in trouble, I've never looked at a trip to the office as a cause for celebration.

When we get to the main office, the door to Mr. Turley's office at the back is closed. Mia and I hesitate, not knowing if he's in there or if he stopped off somewhere on his way from the gym. Mrs. Steeves, the school secretary, looks up from tapping on her computer keyboard.

"Go on in. He's expecting you."

"Sure," I say.

Mia taps on the door and opens it just far enough to peek in. I look over her shoulder and see Mr. Turley hanging up his phone. He waves us in. Mia leads the way and I follow.

"You can close that door, Dominic," he says. His voice sounds tired. I wonder how many phone calls he's either made or taken as this thing unfolds.

As if he could read my mind, he says, "Media. CBC, some newspapers, even CNN in the US—a lot of big ones and a whole lot of smaller ones. But I'm not complaining, you understand. The people who have the toughest job in all this are Farhad and his family. Hey, sorry guys." He points to the two chairs on our side of the desk. "Sit down. Can I get you a water?"

Actually I'd love a water but I'm not sure how long we're going to be there so I shake my head. Mia says, "No, thanks."

"I just wanted to talk to you two because I understand you are Farhad's closest friends."

"I guess so," I mumble.

"Well, a couple of things. First of all, Farhad's going

to need his friends more than he ever has in his life. Some of the stuff that was written on the walls in the pharmacy was directed at him. And as we said in the assembly, it was pretty awful. I've told him to take his time coming back to school but he wants to get back here sooner rather than later. I think he wants to show whoever did this that he's not going to let it change the way he lives his life. So I'm guessing he'll be here tomorrow or the next day."

"That sounds like Farhad," Mia says.

Mr. Turley gives us the same small smile we saw in the gym and nods his head. "I know you two are going to be there for him and I just want you to know that if there's anything I can do to make his return to school and his normal life easier, don't hesitate to ask, okay?"

"Okay," I say.

"The other part of why I wanted to chat with you is trickier. As I said in the gymnasium, the police and the Shirvanis have absolutely no idea who did this. Not yet. It is possible that the people who did this—the police are quite sure it's more than one person—were in the gymnasium just now. I have no idea but that's a possibility."

He shifts his weight in his chair and moves around a bit. It's obvious this is hard for him to say.

"I hope I'm wrong. I hope the people who hate enough to do what I saw in that drugstore this morning are not anyone I know. And I hope that Hastings High isn't about to become famous for all the wrong reasons. But we have to face the reality that the perpetrators could be Hastings students. Because you two are closer to Farhad than anyone in this school you might see something that none of the rest of us sees. If that happens—if you hear or see anything that raises your antennae even a little bit, I hope I can count on you to either call the number you'll be getting from your teacher later this morning or come and talk to me. It's the old adage, 'If you see something, say something.' And please encourage Farhad to do the same thing. If you feel more comfortable talking to the police, that's fine too. I know all of us want to help if we can and I just want you to know that any help you or your friends can give us will be very much appreciated."

By the time Mia and I leave Mr. Turley's office, it's third period. We start in the direction of the chem lab but neither of us is all that into how energy links matter to gravitational, electromagnetic and nuclear forces in the universe.

"Feel like getting a coffee?"

"Yeah, maybe," Mia says and both of us know I'm not talking about the cafeteria and so for the first time in either of our academic careers we decide to cut class. There's a coffee place a couple of blocks from the school and it's only a few minutes before we're sitting on a park bench in a mini park across the street from Grounds Zero, two coffees in hand. Mia's is a dark roast with one milk and mine a regular roast, two milk, no sugar.

For a few minutes we concentrate on sipping our coffee and watching a couple of crows fighting over a Kit Kat wrapper.

"At least they've got good taste in chocolate bars," I say. But neither of us laughs or even smiles. It's like humour is just one of the things that's been turned on its head in the last couple of days.

"This sucks," Mia says after a while.

I stop blowing into my coffee to cool it and nod. "No argument there."

"What do we do?"

I take a small drink and look at her. "I don't know.

I guess it's like Turley said—we need to be there for Farhad and we need to keep an eye out for anything that looks offside as far as how people are treating him." I'm careful to keep my face from showing anything that might indicate I'm thinking about Foster MacLennan.

"Do you know how hard that's going to be? Can you tell the difference between teasing and being racist? People joke with Farhad all the time. *Farhad* jokes all the time. I don't want to be a detective."

"I don't either but I don't think we have to be. I think we'll know if we see something that goes way beyond joking and teasing."

Mia sets her coffee down on the bench. "There are creeps in our school, like there are in every school. But what if we rat somebody out for just being a jerk and they've got nothing to do with what happened at the drugstore?"

"That's for the cops to figure out. Look, don't let this eat you up. We might see nothing."

I can see she's pretty upset. "Listen," I put my hand on her shoulder. "I was a little over the top a few minutes ago. I guess I'm just worried about Farhad. I can't say I've ever seen anything that I thought was totally out of line. There's people that won't talk to Farhad and they look at him like he threw up on their shoes, but there's people who look at me that way too."

"Nice vomit reference," Mia says.

"Thanks," I shrug. "English is my best subject."

This time Mia manages a small laugh.

I stand up. "Maybe we better get back to school before we're the ones being ratted out."

We don't talk much on the way back to school, but as we get to the front door, Mia says, "I just wish we could see Farhad."

"I know. I feel the same way. But I don't know about going over to his house right now. Maybe he just wants to be with his family."

"I hope he's at school tomorrow."

"Yeah, me too."

I pull the door open and we step inside and drop our coffee cups into a big garbage barrel. As we turn around we practically bump into Mr. Turley. Neither of us says anything and for a few seconds neither does Mr. Turley. Then a grin slowly forms on his face.

"Next time you two go to Grounds Zero for a coffee break, bring me back a chocolate chip muffin, okay?"

I nod, a little more vigorously than necessary and Mia says, "Just one?"

"Just one." He chuckles and starts to walk away, then turns back to face us. "By the way, with everything that's been going on, I haven't told you how amazing I thought both of you were in *Wait Until Dark*."

Our "thanks" comes almost in unison.

"You guys okay?"

"Yeah," I say. "We're okay, Mr. Turley."

"Good," he says and turns again, this time disappearing down the hall in the direction of the cafeteria.

11

APRIL 24

The Return

Farhad has come back to school. Mia and I are at the bench waiting and watching and she sees him first.

She runs in his direction but he waves her off and comes to the bench dropping onto it like he's carrying fifty pounds of flour on his shoulder.

"I missed this place," he says, but the grin that's usually on his face is absent. "And you guys too, of course."

I'm guessing he's trying to be funny—to be the old Farhad—but to me it looks half-hearted. He looks thin, his face almost pinched like you see in old people. And tired; he looks really tired.

"How you doin', Buddy?" I give his shoulder a pat.

He looks at me but doesn't say anything and for a second I think he might cry but he doesn't. He also

David A. Poulsen

doesn't respond to my question with more than a shrug.

"It's going to be okay," I say and as soon as the words are out of my mouth I realize they're pathetic—like a badly scripted line in a reality TV show. Farhad obviously feels the same way.

"Dom, the first thing you're going to have to learn is not to talk to me like I'm somebody's puppy or cute little brother. I'm me, the same me I was before some creeps tried to put my family out of business and scare us into running away. We're not scared, at least not scared enough. We're staying here and we're going to live our lives the same way we always have. So the first thing I need from my friends is to be the same way you've always been."

"Check," I say. "But it's good to have you back even if you are a pain in the ass."

Farhad nods and says, "That's better. Now let's go to school. I want to get even smarter than I already am."

As we head for the school we're all smiling but I still feel that the joking around and speech about being the same as we've always been is kind of forced, kind of fake. We're not the same. Especially Farhad. Something happened that has changed us or at least changed the way we look at the world around us. He's doing all he can to make us all think none of this matters but I'm not buying it. I know Farhad better than anyone does, except maybe his family, and I can see it. In his eyes, in the way he walks, in his voice. I'm not sure I know the word for it but it's hard to watch it happening to a friend.

As we get to the front door, a big Grade 12 kid butts in front of us and pushes Farhad out of the way. I look at Mia and she shakes her head. And she's right. There's a difference between racism and just being rude and I'm going to have to work at not overreacting to stuff that doesn't matter.

We step inside and my phone pings. I pull it out of my jacket pocket and look at the screen. Then I look again. Classic double take. The text is from Callie. All it says is:

> *Hey Dom*
> *Wanted to say hi,*
> *So hi and have a great day*
> *Callie.*

For a minute my mind isn't thinking about Farhad or racist attacks or anything but the girl I first saw in the window of the house at 624 Edmund Avenue.

———————————

By the end of the school day it's starting to feel a little more normal again. Farhad is kind of subdued (for him) in most of the classes but the teachers operate like he missed a few days with a cold or the flu—careful not to draw attention to his being back.

I guess that's probably the best way to handle it; I know that's the way Farhad wants it—I know that because he just told us that again out here at the bench. We don't get to discuss it for very long because Mr. Shirvani gets here with his Audi a little quicker, actually a *lot* quicker, than usual. Maybe he's worried about Farhad being at school any longer than he has to be, I don't know, but it's a quiet ride home ... no laughing, not much talking at all and a lot of Mr. Shirvani looking in his rear-view mirror at Farhad and me in the back seat. Mia's in the front seat and I don't know if she's finding the atmosphere as, I don't know, maybe tense, as I am. She looks at her phone almost the whole way to her house and jumps out of the car with barely a wave as she heads for her front door.

After she's gone, I look over at Farhad who's staring

out the side window at the same houses we go by every day. Except it's like he really needs to study them for some reason. I think it's mostly so he won't have to talk to me. And that's when I realize something. He's scared. And so is Mr. Shirvani. Whatever happened in their store, whatever happened *to* their store has really shaken both of them. And, yes, they are scared. Two people that I'm pretty sure don't get that way all that easily are scared as hell.

I know I can't ask what it is that's got to them. And it bugs me that I don't feel like I'm really helping them at all. My best friend and my best friend's dad are hurting and I'm sitting here in the backseat of their car like a lump of useless clay.

And I hate it.

We get to my house without actually saying a single word from Mia's house on. I look over at Farhad again. "Hey, you feel like hangin' at my place? My mom can give you a ride home when she gets here."

He shakes his head. "I have to help my dad at the store."

I look to the front seat and Mr. Shirvani is suddenly busy looking for something in the glove compartment. And once again I'm very aware that these two people are very different from how they were, even *who* they were, just a few days before.

And that makes me so angry at whoever did this to them that I just want to punch something. But I climb out of the car instead.

"Thanks for the ride, Mr. Shirvani." And then to Farhad. "See you at the bench in the morning."

He manages a half-smile and an almost-nod as I close the door and head for the house.

———————————————

A whole week goes by with not a lot happening. Mr. Shirvani hired a couple of guys to do the repairs that were necessary after the vandalism of the drugstore. Farhad told me that some of their work involved painting over the graffiti that was plastered over a couple of the walls. He also told me he wouldn't repeat what was actually written. I don't blame him.

At school no one has jumped out as the likely suspects or even as someone who might want to get on the anti-Muslim bandwagon. I guess I've been paying more attention to how people treat Farhad but so far

I can't say I've seen anything I'd call suspicious. Some people smile and stop and talk to him, some give him unpleasant, even nasty looks and others walk by and don't notice him at all—exactly the way it was before all this happened. Or at least the way I *think* it was before all this happened.

I've tried calling Callie a couple of times, got her voice mail and left a message. She hasn't called me back ... at least not yet. Mia is going to an audition for a play that's being put on by that semi-professional theatre group, but she's been pretty low-key about it. I think she's trying hard to keep it real around Farhad and me.

I guess the most painful indication that the ugliness hasn't gone away happened yesterday in math class. We got some tests back that we'd written a couple of days before and Farhad got 48%. That's not Farhad. He's not a math genius but I don't think he's ever failed a test, or even been close, in all the time I've known him. For him to get 48% means he's having a whole lot of trouble concentrating on schoolwork right now. I guess that's natural.

What was worse was how he reacted. Or more accurately, how he didn't react. No change of expression

David A. Poulsen

on his face, his eyes kind of blank ... empty. Not really with it. I felt bad for him but again didn't really know what to say or do.

I got 79% on the test but I didn't even mention that to Farhad. I don't think he would have cared anyway. It's like Farhad the Joker left town and has been replaced by a more serious, sadder guy who wears the same clothes but doesn't really know how to laugh.

And today, I'm sitting at the bench alone. Mia texted me that she had a meeting with a teacher after school and would be about fifteen minutes. No word from Farhad. No sign of Farhad. He was in school—we had lunch, not much actual talking except from Mia. But he's not here now and I'm worried about it. I don't really know anything about depression but I'm starting to wonder if that might be going on with Farhad. He hasn't talked about all the girls that are crazy about him ... not once since the attack on the store. He doesn't say anything funny or totally stupid like he always did. And he doesn't laugh if somebody else is funny.

If it is depression, what should I be doing? I think Farhad knows that I'm there for him and that I'm his friend through whatever happens. I think he also knows that what happened to him and his family makes me sick. Sick and angry.

But maybe that's not enough. Maybe I should be actually trying to *do* something. Trouble is I don't what it is I should be doing. And another thought, a really scary one, has crossed my mind a few times. Should I be worried about suicide? I mean I can't believe that suicide could enter his head for even a minute. But you hear the stories all the time. I just wish I knew more.

———————

Birthdays have never been a big deal to me. I mean I like cake, and getting presents is fun but other than that I could just skip that day altogether and go on to the next one—birthday plus one.

But this one's different. First of all, there's the whole turning sixteen thing which is kind of a big deal. Mom's actually planned a sort-of-party; I mean it's not like a bunch of kids are coming over to eat cake, give me presents and play pin the tail on the donkey. I guess it's Mom's idea of what a party for an almost grown-up should be. She's taking Mia and Farhad and me to a restaurant for dinner—she knows I like Italian so we're doing Ye Olde Spaghetti Factory in the city. And to be honest I think that should be an okay time.

But of course, the really big deal about this birthday is that I can get my license and start driving the Satin Wagon to school. Yeah, I know, this is the same car that a few months ago was the thing in my life I hated most but I've been working on it every spare minute and I have to say it's looking—and even sounding—pretty good.

I've minimized the belching smoke issue—with a little help from Mr. Barstad who is pretty good with cars. And the rattle that's bugged me for like—ever— is pretty much gone. I figured that one out by myself. And the interior even smells pretty good. Mr. Barstad also helped get one ugly dent out of the front left fender and I touched up a couple of small rust spots with spray paint. Okay, it isn't the car everybody gathers around in the school parking lot and goes *Oooh, sweet ride.* But it also isn't the car that makes people laugh whenever they see it.

And I'm pumped. I take my test the day after tomorrow—I plan to pass it first time—and then it's me picking up Mia and Farhad and heading for school and home again after. How cool is that?

And, of course there's always the chance that Callie might be a passenger in there one day. I'm hoping she's not used to a Jag or something. Actually I've thought about that. The "murder" house that she lived in is nothing special. And she was willing to talk to a guy who was riding his bike. So I'm hoping she comes from a family that wouldn't look down their noses at a 1981 Plymouth Reliant Station Wagon.

The murder house. That gets me thinking. I haven't heard anything about what's going on with that. Maybe there's some investigation still happening but if there is I haven't learned anything. And, of course, I haven't exactly spent a lot of time with Callie so I haven't been able to ask her about it. Maybe that will happen soon too, now that I've got my own car.

Yeah, those are sweet words.

My. Own. Car.

12

APRIL 27

The Importance of Carbs

The Satin Wagon runs perfectly for three days. Okay, maybe *perfectly* is a bit of an overstatement. But the point is it actually functions for three amazing days—three days of me driving around town with my license (first try) in my pocket and a large grin on my face waving to everyone I know. And quite a few people I don't know.

On day four the carburetor stops doing whatever it is carburetors do. It's deader than the people in Thomas Gray's poem. I have enough money to pay for one maybe two Big Macs which leaves me a little short of what I need to have the carburetor repaired. I don't feel good about asking Mr. Barstad for any more help and I can't ask Mom for the money—not after she just gave me the car as a present. So that leaves me back on my bike, which, after being behind the wheel of the Satin Wagon for three days, is a major letdown.

Normally I'd be spilling my sorrows to Farhad but I can't do that either. Partly because Farhad has stopped showing up at the bench and for rides home. And he barely talks to us during the day. I don't think he's mad, at least not at Mia and me, but it's like the world that Farhad knew has been blown apart and he's not sure he wants to be part of the one that's replaced it.

I'm still trying to be there if he feels like talking or even if he just wants to hang out without talking. And he's not rude. It's just that he's so damn distant and I don't know what to do. I know Mia feels the same way because she spent twenty minutes after school yesterday telling me that.

"By the way," she said, "not to change the subject but where's your car? I thought you two were joined at the fender."

"Yeah, well, there's no problem with the fenders but there is with the carburetor—at least I think that's it. Anyway the Satin Wagon is on vacation for the time being."

"Hnh," was all she said and then she started typing

on her phone keypad which I thought was kind of rude especially since she had been a Satin Wagon passenger right up until it died its horrible death.

"Don't lose any sleep over it," I said. "I'm sure I'll have another car in ten years or so." I hoped my sarcasm was making her feel terrible but she typed on, pausing only to read what I guessed were responses, probably from her Hollywood agents. That's when she surprised me.

"Can you get it towed?"

"What?"

"Towed ... you know ... ee-ee-ee ..." Her winching sounds were pathetic and I would have laughed but I was busy trying to figure out what she was talking about.

"I guess so," I said. "Why are you asking me that?"

"My sister—you've never met her, she's nine years older than me—she's a mechanic, works at Starlight Auto on Dawson Road on the other side of town. She says if you can get it there, she'll fix it and just charge you for the parts, unless it needs a motor rebuild or something."

"Naw, I googled what it was doing and I'm pretty sure it's the carburetor."

"You googled."

"Yeah."

"I'm sure that's what all the real mechanics do." Her sarcasm was even more obvious than mine. "Anyway if you get it to her, she'll look at it, with actual tools and everything. You know, if Google fails to fix it."

"Your sister's a mechanic."

"And a really good one."

"Wow," I said, "that is so cool."

"What's cool about it? I hope you're not one of those guys who thinks that there are *guy* jobs—stuff that women couldn't possibly do."

"No ... uh ... no," I stammered. "I just meant first of all I didn't know you had a sister, and secondly I didn't know you had a sister who's a mechanic, and thirdly ... well, there is no thirdly."

I didn't pursue it because Mia was obviously in the mood to argue no matter what I said but I thought it really was cool that her sister was a mechanic. What was even cooler was that Mom has some Auto Club or Association membership which meant the towing was free and Mia's sister had my car repaired and ready to go in a couple of hours. (Oh, and by the way, doubters, it *was* the carburetor).

And that's why I'm sitting here right now—behind

the wheel of my car staring at my phone and a message from Callie that says:

> *Hey there*
>
> *Are you ever going to ask me out?*

Actually, it's a pretty good question. I've been asking myself that same thing for several days and the answer hasn't exactly leaped into my head. Truth is I know the answer. I was afraid she wouldn't like my car. Even with the stuff that's been done to make the Satin Wagon presentable, I was afraid she'd only see the rust and smoke and miss some of the stuff I was kind of proud of ... like the almost-new speakers I got from a guy at school. I put them in myself, fired up some Tom Petty and the Heartbreakers and Ed Sheeran (old school– new school) and it sounded amazing. Then there are the almost-new seat covers; yes, I know, the front seat and back seat covers are supposed to match and mine don't— but they're still pretty good. And then there's the new carburetor. And it actually *is* new. And it was installed by a female mechanic; that's gotta be worth something. Oh, by the way, the bill was $84. Mom loaned me the money and said she'd take a buck a week off my allowance until I've paid it back. Which means I should have the thing paid off before my 18th birthday.

Of course, if Callie doesn't see that stuff ... or doesn't care, then I'm kind of hooped. So I haven't asked her out, which I realize is just stupid. I'm still thinking about that when I get a second text and this one really has me thinking.

I need a favour.

I stare at my phone. Is the favour asking her out? Or something completely different? I'm thinking the favour is a different deal altogether. Only one way to find out.

Sure, if I can

What do u need?

I don't have to wait long for an answer.

Meet for coffee?

I'll explain then.

The mystery girl is mysterious again.

Sure ... when ... where?

This time a little time goes by. Maybe she's thinking about her schedule or something.

Tomorrow. After school.

Vinnie's?

Perfect. I've been thinking I should cruise Vinnie's

in the Satin Wagon anyway, you know, just to let the place's regulars check out the wheels.

Sure. See u then.

She sends a heart back to me which I figure is a good sign. But the whole favour thing really has me thinking. First the reminder about asking her out, then she wants me to do her a favour. Tomorrow is going to be a very interesting day. I just hope it's interesting in a good way.

13

APRIL 28

Callie

Showered, shaved and shampooed.

Yes, I shave. Okay, maybe not every day—more like once a week. But this morning I decided to advance my shaving schedule by a few days, you know, just to be sure.

Callie and I agreed to meet at Vinnie's at 4:30. I've been here since a quarter to four, sitting outside in the Satin Wagon (which also received extra attention for the occasion) and looking from my watch to the entrance to Vinnie's ... and back to my watch again.

The minutes tick by at about the same speed that you spread frozen peanut butter. I alternate between having the air-conditioning blasting to alleviate the sweat factor and turning on the heat because I get so cold from the air-conditioning. Has there ever been anyone more pathetic?

At 4:25 I get out of the car. I don't want to keep her waiting.

At 4:26 I get back in the car. I don't want to seem too eager.

At 4:29 I get out of the car again and this time I actually cross the road and walk through the entrance and into Vinnie's. But then I'm struck by another bout of panic. What do I do now that I'm in here—look around for her? Will that seem desperate? Or just saunter over to a seat all totally cool and sit down like meeting gorgeous women in Vinnie's is something that happens all the time and frankly it's a bit boring. Or maybe—

I don't get to ponder the question any further because Callie is leaning against the wall just inside the door. She's texting but looks up just as I walk in, drops her phone into her purse and smiles at me. She's wearing canary yellow jogging pants and a matching warmup jacket like she's either just finished a workout or is going to start one after she leaves Vinnie's.

I'm about to ask her how she managed to get into the place without me seeing her but then I figure I'd be telling her I've been sitting outside watching the door, a totally dweeb move. Instead I say, "Great to see you" and we share a hug that's more like a man-hug than anything.

"Come on." She smiles at me. "There's a booth near the back."

I follow her to the booth and slide in across from her. I'm trying to keep my face under control but I'm not sure it's working. I keep thinking of that Cheshire Cat in *Alice in Wonderland*—you know, the Disney animated one—and hoping that's not what I look like.

The server is a girl I know from school; I think her name is Georgia or maybe Nevada, anyway I'm pretty sure it's a state. I don't know her well but she has a reputation of being a major gossip and she's not that well liked. She stares hard at Callie the whole time we're ordering, which isn't long since Callie wants only a diet Pepsi and I settle for coffee.

"It feels like it's been a really long time since I've seen you," Callie says after the server leaves.

"That's because it *has* been a long time," I tell her. "Opening night of the play."

She laughs. "I guess you're right. Did I tell you I thought you were great?"

"Actually you did which was a lie, but it was nice of you to say it anyway."

She smiles at me. "Well, it wasn't a big lie. You were pretty good."

I return the smile. "Thanks ... I think."

"And you still haven't asked me out yet."

I'm still working on my answer to that when— Dakota, that's it, Dakota—returns, sets our drinks down and says, "Anything else?" in a tone of voice that lets us know that what she's really saying is, *I hope you don't want anything else.*

Callie says, "I'm good for now, thanks," and I shake my head. Dakota moves off but not very far and starts wiping the hell out of a table that doesn't look like it needs it.

Callie and I watch her for a while, thinking she'll leave soon except she doesn't. After at least a minute, I say, "Hey Dakota, you'd be able to hear better if you cleaned *our* table."

She stomps off and I'm pretty sure I hear the word "asshole" as she disappears around a corner.

Callie and I are both grinning as I stir my coffee and she pops a straw into her glass.

"Yeah, about that, I ... uh ..."

She waves her hand at me. "It's okay. Actually I just wanted you to know it'll be a little easier now. My mom and I are moving back into the house on Edmund."

"Six twenty-four?"

"Uh-huh. For a while Mom didn't like the idea of living there anymore but she's changed her mind and we're moving back home. I'm kind of glad. And next year I'll be going to Hastings."

"Really? That's awesome." I realize I sound like I'm twelve as I say that. "I mean, well, that will be ... uh ... great." There are days when I wonder how it's possible that English is my best subject as I stumble along trying unsuccessfully to find the right words. It would be so much better if I could write everything out before I had to say it but apparently that's not how conversation works.

For a couple of minutes, Callie and I concentrate on our drinks but I finally set my cup down and look at her.

"What?"

"I know it's probably none of my business and you don't have to tell me if you don't want to but I was wondering ... what actually happened in that house. I mean, like I said, you don't have to ..."

She leans forward, and puts her fingers gently against my mouth and shakes her head. "That's partly why I wanted to meet you here—I want to tell you what happened."

I nod and don't say anything; I just wait.

She takes a sip of her drink and looks at her hands for a while then finally up at me.

"I mean it wouldn't be right if we're dating and I don't tell you something as important as that."

I almost point out that technically we're not dating but I decide silence is my best option at that exact moment.

"There were five of us living there, my mom and dad and me and two guys who were friends of my dad. The three of them, my dad and those two guys—who were brothers—were dealing drugs. Not out of the house; they have another place, I'm not exactly sure where. It wasn't a great place to live since those two moved in with us. There was a third brother, younger, maybe our age, but he wasn't there that much, lived somewhere else with his mom, I think. Anyway there were lots of arguments and yelling and stuff whenever those two were around. Mom was pretty scared even though they left her and me pretty much alone.

"Anyway the night of the shooting there wasn't any of the arguing and hollering. My dad was at home and it was just the three of us. It was one of the few times we were like a normal family. Mom and I cooked a really nice dinner and Dad was joking around and we were listening to music and just talking, kind of like it was when I was little and we lived in Colorado. It was actually fun except that in a home like we had, you were never totally relaxed. You never knew when the brothers might show up and as soon as that happened Dad would change. He wasn't mean to us, not really, but he was just so … tense, so nervous, like he was in their power or something. It was like my real dad had gone away."

I know about dads going away and have a pretty good idea what she's feeling. But I don't say anything. I think it's better right now to let her talk.

She takes a sip of her soft drink and a couple of deep breaths.

"But we were just talking about music and stuff—my dad's actually a pretty smart guy—and Mom was in the kitchen getting out this dessert thing she'd made. And suddenly the two brothers—Shane and Jackie Krebs—they burst into the house like it was on fire and they were there to rescue us. They were all out of breath and their faces were sweaty and they were both dirty, like they'd been rolling around in something.

"At first they didn't say anything; they just stood there looking at us sitting at the table having dinner like real people and then Jackie, he's the older one and even crazier than Shane, said to my dad, 'We gotta talk, man, we gotta talk right now.'

"I was hoping Dad would tell them to get lost or something but he didn't. He just kind of shrugged his shoulders and the three of them went into the bedroom where the brothers slept and pretty soon they were talking really loud. I didn't feel like listening to them so I gave up on the dinner and went outside and that's when I saw you. I'd seen you before in the lane between the house and McCloy's and I was really excited that I'd actually get to talk to you, but then my dad called me and I had to go back inside."

"Yeah, I was really wanting to talk to you too."

She nods and smiles before resuming her story. "When I got back in the house there was more yelling and everyone was mad at everyone else. My mom and I went downstairs to where my bedroom is and closed the door and waited for it all to settle down. But it didn't settle down. I don't know when it was exactly but maybe a half-hour or an hour later, we heard two gunshots. We didn't know they were gunshots at the time—just these loud booms. At first I thought it was a door slamming or somebody hitting the wall with something like a baseball bat. Stupid, I guess, but I wasn't thinking *gun*. Mom and I were really scared and I kept thinking somebody would kick the door to my bedroom open and come in there, but nobody did and finally it got really quiet in the house."

"That had to be really scary for you and your mom."

"It was," she nodded. "After a while longer, Mom and I came out of my room. We went upstairs and my dad was sort of crying and trying to talk but none of what he was saying made any sense. He was packing a suitcase but he was so ... weird. I didn't know if it was because he was so upset or maybe he was on something but he kept putting stuff in and then taking it out again. Mom tried to get him to tell us what had happened but it was hopeless. All I could make out was 'I have to get out of here.' He must have said that twenty times."

Callie stops and takes another sip of her soft drink.

David A. Poulsen

Then she reaches across and takes hold of both my hands. Her hands are cold and they're shaking. We hold hands like that for a while but I don't say anything. I'm not sure what I can say that will make her feel better so for a couple of minutes we just sit, totally still and quiet, holding hands and looking at each other.

"Do you think this is weird?"

"What?"

"You know, that we're sitting here holding hands and I'm telling you all this stuff and we hardly know each other?"

"No ... I mean, not really ... well, I guess, okay, yeah, maybe it's a *little*, um, different."

She nods slowly and looks down. "Yeah."

"But it's okay. I mean it's not like it's creepy weird or anything. I guess we both just ... uh ... like each other, right? And I do want to hear whatever you want to tell me, whether you just tell me as a friend or as ... something else."

She nods again and gives me a half-smile. Then she starts talking again. "So Dad threw a couple more things in his suitcase and closed it up. Then he started for the door. Mom ran over and stopped him and I can't remember exactly what she said but she wanted to know what was wrong and why he was so panicked. And she asked him how long he'd be gone. But he didn't answer, not really; he just looked at us and I've never seen anyone look so scared. Then just like that he was out the door and gone. Mom went outside after him and called to him but he jumped in his pickup and raced off like ... like ... I don't know, he was just gone.

"Mom and I sat on the couch and she was shaking her head over and over. We didn't say much or cry or anything. We didn't know what to do; none of it made any sense. Finally Mom said she'd make us some tea and she went into the kitchen, well, not all the way into the kitchen. She only got as far as the doorway and then she started screaming. I ran to her but she turned and tried to stop me from actually going into the kitchen. But I saw ..."

Callie stops and I see the tears and she's shaking harder now. I'm not sure what to do or say. Should I encourage her to finish telling me what happened that night or leave it up to her? She's still holding my hands and now she's squeezing them really hard. I can tell all of this is really tough for her to relive.

I lean forward. "You don't have to tell me any more if you don't want to."

She shakes her head. "This is the first time I've talked about it with anybody except the police. Not even with my mom. We haven't talked about it since that night."

I nod. "You know I'll do anything I can to help, right?"

Her shoulders move up and down just a little. "I'm not sure what you can do. I don't know what anyone can do. I'm just glad you're here, that you're listening to me." She pauses for a minute, then goes on. "When I ran to my mom I saw what she was looking at. There was someone lying on the kitchen floor. There was blood everywhere. For some reason I didn't scream. Mom and I just stood there holding onto each other and then we moved away from the kitchen ... from the body. Because I was pretty sure it *was* a body. With all that blood I figured the guy had to be dead. He was lying face down and his head was turned away from me so I didn't know who it was except I remembered the hoodie he was wearing, Shane I mean. He'd been wearing a Blue Jays hoodie and the guy on the floor ... I thought it must be him.

"Mom called the police and we found out later that it *was* Shane. And I guess that's it. The police haven't arrested anyone and we haven't heard from Dad since that night."

"Damn, this has to have been so tough for you and your mom. Are you going to be okay moving back into that house?"

"I don't know." She shakes her head. "Mom says we've got no choice. The house is paid for and we can't afford to keep paying rent somewhere else. The police told us it's okay and they'll be doing drive-bys to check that we're safe and everything. I mean I can't see how we'd be in any danger. It's not like we saw anything, like we were witnesses or anything. And if my dad ... I mean ... if he comes back home ... I know he wouldn't hurt us. He's not like that; he's ..."

She stops talking then. No tears, just the saddest face I've ever seen looking down at our hands.

"Yeah, I guess so," I say, which I know even as I'm saying it is next to useless.

"Anyway, I just want my life to get back to being sort of normal."

That's twice I've heard that recently, first from Farhad and now from Callie, both of them involved in something totally horrible.

"I get that," I tell her. "So like I said, anything I can do to help, I hope you know, I'd like to do what I can."

She smiles and lets go of my hands. Even though I realize it's not really a romantic thing, I wouldn't mind if she'd just keep holding onto me.

"Can I tell you something?" She almost whispers it.

"Sure."

"I almost didn't come to the play. I wasn't sure watching a play with murders and stuff was going to be all that great right then. But the counsellor at my school said I should try to do normal things as long as I felt like it. I'm glad I was there that night. And it was so cool watching you up there on stage."

"I'm glad you were there too. I guess it *was* a pretty scary play, especially at the end. And especially after everything that's happened to you."

"Sometimes it feels like I'm in a play too ... that none of this is real. I wish the curtain would close and I could just go back to having my old life again." She smiles at me. "Well, maybe not everything about my old life."

I smile and nod but the whole thing is still bothering me. "I don't know ... I just worry about you moving back into that house, I mean if your dad—"

She interrupts me and she's angry. "My dad didn't kill Shane Krebs, okay? I know that."

"Okay," I say, "I just meant with the killer still out there somewhere, it just seems—"

She stops me again. "I told you we *have* to. Mom can't afford to pay for a place when we have somewhere we can live that won't cost us much."

Maybe she realizes she sounded a little harsh and her voice turns softer. "I appreciate that you're worried about me. But we'll be okay. Really."

I nod again. Maybe I've read too many murder mysteries or something but the idea of her and her mom back in that house is stressing me out. I realize that I've said all I can say without totally pissing off a girl I care about. So I shut up. Well, actually I change the subject.

"Did you ever meet Farhad, the guy who did sound and lights for the play?"

"I think so. He talked to me that night I came to the play. He talked ... a lot."

I laugh and Callie does too. "Yeah, that sounds like Farhad. He thinks every girl is in love with him. He's actually a fun guy. At least he was."

Callie looks at me. "Was?"

I tell her the story of the vandalizing of Farhad's family's drugstore and the racial stuff that was written on the walls.

"That's disgusting."

"Yeah it is. It's totally changed Farhad and I can't really blame him. I just feel bad that two people I care about are having a pretty rough time."

We sit for a while and pretend we're not looking at each other even though we are. I swallow and then I swallow again. "So I was thinking … wondering, I mean … if you'd … uh … like to go out with me?"

She smiles and looks at me. "Well, I don't know. I mean is this like, *Let's do lunch sometime*, or did you have something more definite in mind?"

"Oh, definitely something more definite. I was thinking next Saturday night." That gives me over a week to … um … get ready. "I haven't been to that new movieplex yet, but it's supposed to be a pretty cool place; they serve you food right in your seat and everything."

"I know," she says. "I've been a couple of times; it's a fun place."

I guess I'm a little disappointed that she's been there before and for a second I wonder if it was with a guy but then I realize it would be pretty stupid to be jealous when we haven't even gone out yet.

"I heard there are four different movies. How about I text you what's on and we can decide which one to go to?"

"Perfect."

She stands up and we move out of the booth. I suddenly realize I have a difficult decision to make. I mean how do you say goodbye to somebody who kissed you once already? Even if it was just a congratulations kiss ... anyway while I'm thinking about this, Callie steps closer and gives me a hug. I'm careful not to turn it into one of those creepy way-too-long hugs but at the same time I don't want her to think I'm not into hugging because I am. Anyway we hug and I think it's going okay and then she's gone.

Even with all the talk about the shooting at 624 Edmund Avenue, I'm suddenly in a very good mood—it's a little early to think of Callie as my girlfriend but hey, we are going out and that's cause for a good mood. So good, in fact, that I sit back down and order myself fries and gravy. I even smile at Dakota. Ah, nothing like junk food to make a good moment great.

14

MAY 1

Farhad

It's Monday morning and I'm still in an upbeat mood when I get to the bench. I'm the first one there, and then Mia races up, all excited about this play she went to with her parents on Saturday night. It was a musical. I don't catch the name, mainly because I'm not listening. After all, I think my news is way more exciting.

I don't get to tell her about Callie and me though because Farhad arrives right then and he's in a totally opposite mood from Mia and me. He is pissed, *really* pissed.

"Hey Dude," I say, "'s happenin'?" I'm still trying to figure out how to talk to the guy since the incident at the drugstore. Serious but not too serious? Sort of goofball ... what?

"What's happening is that I just came from my locker

and you might notice I'm not carrying a binder or a backpack or any books."

"Yeah, what's with that?" For a second I think maybe he's quit school.

"The reason is I don't have any of those things anymore."

Mia says, "What are you talking about?"

"Somebody broke into my locker. Cut the lock and cleaned out my locker except for the garbage and crap I had in there. Everything else, textbooks, school jacket, brand new trainers—gone."

"What?" Mia practically screams it.

I'm almost as loud. "Are you kidding me? Come on." I know how excited Farhad was about those shoes. Nike Air Max 97s.

"Oh, and just to make sure this wasn't a random hit on just any locker, they decorated the inside of my locker door with a picture of a guy and a camel—I'm not going to say what they're doing but you can guess. And there was pretty much the same message written on the back wall of the locker that was splashed all over our drugstore walls."

For a minute I've got nothing. I can't believe that this kind of crap can happen. I don't *want to* believe

David A. Poulsen

that this kind of crap can happen. In our school. And then it hits me. If the message in Farhad's locker is the same one that was in the drugstore, then it's likely the same people. And more and more it's looking like those people are Hastings students.

"That sucks, man." It's weak and I know that as I'm saying it, but I don't know what else to say.

Farhad doesn't answer me. I can see that he's mad and I get that but there are also some tears. Angry tears, sad tears, it doesn't matter. I'm pretty sure I've never seen the guy cry. Mia steps up and puts her arms around Farhad. She's crying too. I put my hand on his shoulder and I feel it shaking. The three of us just stand there—angry, sad and for me at least, still wishing I could figure out what I should be doing for my best friend. And to stop the hate that looks more and more like it's part of what Hastings High is.

———————

School's been pretty much a write-off since Farhad's news this morning. I was next to useless in my first couple of classes and I didn't even suit up for gym class which normally I love. I faked an injury—*faked an injury*, for God's sake—something I swore I'd never do. So, yeah the day hasn't exactly been a winner. Except for English, which is where I am right now.

I'm sitting here staring at the test I completely forgot about—the test on "Elegy Written in a Country Churchyard." We finished that unit last week and I really meant to study my notes and at least read the poem again for the test.

Except I forgot. It might have something to do with spending most of last night thinking about Callie and the murder that happened at 624 Edmund Avenue. But I doubt that Ms. Lathrop is going to cut me much slack because of that.

I haven't actually read any of the questions or even looked at the test until right now and for a second I want to get up and run to the front of the classroom and give Ms. Lathrop a hug. Thing is, the test is one question and it's not really even a question. What we have to do is write a few stanzas for the poem as if we were Thomas Gray. It can go anywhere in the poem but it has to follow the themes Gray was writing about and it has to be at least three four-line stanzas using the same rhyme scheme Gray used.

David A. Poulsen

Perfect. I know I can nail this.

I decide to make my three stanzas—twelve lines—about one guy who's buried in the churchyard. I give the guy a name—William Colley—and I make him the caretaker of the church. And the guy who dug a lot of the graves. Now he's in one. So I just have to write about his life and how he died at age forty-seven—people often didn't live all that long back then.

But what do I say about the guy? There has to be a reason that Gray (or I) would write about him. And then it hits me. There are people in the community (Stoke Poges) who don't like him, maybe even hate him because he's different. Not from another country or anything like that—maybe the guy's poor and uneducated. Maybe he's dirty a lot of the time from digging and being in all that dirt and he doesn't spend a lot of time washing and being clean and stuff. So, there are people—not everybody, just some people—who can't stand William Colley.

Okay, I like the idea; now I just have to write it. How hard can that be?

———————————

I'm back at the bench and I'm feeling pretty good about myself. I don't know if my poem was any good but I know I did a whole lot better than I thought I would when Ms. Lathrop was handing out the test that I'd forgotten about. Mia is upbeat too because she knows she can write poetry. But Farhad is still down.

Okay, maybe down is not an accurate description. Mostly he's just flat ... lifeless.

"How do you think you did on the poem?" I ask.

For a while he just looks at me like maybe I've just asked the stupidest question ever, but finally he shrugs his shoulders. "Who gives a damn?" he says. "Who actually gives a damn?" Then he walks away leaving Mia and me to watch him go.

"I'm really worried about him," Mia says.

I nod but I don't have a lot to add. I'm worried too but I'm starting to think that worrying isn't enough. It feels like we actually have to *do* something.

But what?

15

MAY 8

Mia

Before I get to the Mia stuff, I figure if you're reading this you'll probably want to know how the date went. In a word—it was amazing—no, that's the word people use for everything so how about unbelievable ... uh, that doesn't really work either because it could be unbelievably good or unbelievably bad, so let's settle for stupendous. Yeah, that's a word that doesn't come up all the time—in fact, I'm not sure when I last used it, maybe never, so stupendous it is.

Callie caught a ride to the theatre with her mom who was going to visit a friend nearby which meant Callie wouldn't get to experience the Satin Wagon until after the movie. I got there first but this time I didn't hang around in my car watching the theatre like some guy in a bad spy novel. I was in the lobby ... foyer ... whatever they call the place at the front of the theatre and I have to say I was pretty relaxed.

When Callie got there we bought a couple of snacks—Callie's a pretty healthy eater so that ruled out buttered popcorn and chocolate bars. We settled for these iced fruit bar things which were actually really good. We talked it over ahead of time and decided not to go with the delivered food which can be a little expensive. The movie was *Blinded by the Light* (decided by text ahead of time), and it was excellent. At least Callie and I both thought so. Neither of us had seen it when it first came out a couple of years before. For me the music of Bruce Springsteen was the best part. The only downer was that the main character was Pakistani which got me thinking about Farhad and I had trouble staying with the story and not letting my mind wander off to think about my best friend's trouble.

But the movie really was great and the evening just kept getting better. The pizza at Vinnie's was one of the best I'd ever had but that might have had a lot to do with who was sitting on the other side of the pizza. Our conversation was what my dad used to call teenage talk. No discussion of murder or racist jerks at school or anything even close to "depressingly serious." We talked about our favourite groups—Callie's is Fall Out Boy and mine is Nickelback. The good part was I don't hate her favourite group and she doesn't hate mine. I don't know what I would have done if she'd said Ted Nugent or something.

Then, finally, Callie and I were in the Satin Wagon and cruising the downtown like you see in those old movies. We talked about a lot of stuff, gassed up at McCloy's and shared a bottle of root beer while we were driving. While we were rolling down Arnold Avenue, a cool street in town with a lot of fun shops and restaurants, I had the radio on, and what song comes on but Nickelback's *Photograph*. I knew all the words and Callie knew most of them, and we sang like we were Chad himself. Then when it was time to drop her off, the kiss was slow and warm and long, the perfect kiss to end the perfect night.

———————————

Anyway this chapter is supposed to be about Mia and it is. I get to the bench after a pretty good school day. I'm getting kind of used to Farhad missing bench time—

sometimes several days in a row. And when he does show up, he's often pretty unhappy. Today's no different except that when he gets there, just a couple of minutes after me, he's not so much depressed as he is pissed off. A lot of talking to himself under his breath, some swearing, clenched fists, kicking at the pavement ... yeah definite anger. I'm thinking the bad guys— whoever they are—have struck again, done something that's got Farhad fuming.

It's probably a full minute before he acknowledges the fact that I'm there.

"I hope you weren't part of that crap."

I look at him trying to figure out what he's talking about. "Part of what crap? Oh, and by the way, hello, how are you Farhad? Great, thanks, yourself, Dom? How was your day?"

He glares at me for a long time, looking like he's trying to work something out in his mind. "You mean you didn't hear? I seriously thought you were part of it."

"Part of what? Can you just tell me what exactly it was that obviously wrecked your day big time?"

And he's about to, or at least I think he is except that Mia arrives right then and flops down next to me. There's a little smile on her face and she looks, I don't know, expectant. She's sort of watching Farhad, but trying to look like she's not watching him. Like she's waiting for him to do or say something. She doesn't have to wait long.

"That was bullshit."

The smile disappears off Mia's face. "Wait ... what?"

"Absolute crap." Farhad's voice is loud enough that people downtown can likely hear him. "Who do you think you are? And *what* do you think I am? Some charity case?"

I hold up my hands. "Could somebody please stop yelling long enough to tell me what we're talking about here?"

Farhad answers but he doesn't take his accusing eyes off Mia.

"Miss *Aren't I Helpful* and a couple of her friends decided I needed to be looked after. Filled my locker with a new school jacket and new Nike trainers. Like I couldn't afford to buy that stuff myself, like I'm some kind of street person. A let's-help-out-the-brown-kid-and-make-ourselves-feel-good charity case."

He pulls the new shoes out of his backpack and throws them into the trash can that sits a few feet from the bench.

Mia stands up but for a few seconds she doesn't say anything and the two of them are trying to stare down the other like they hate each other. I'm actually afraid one of them is going to slap the other.

"What an ass ... hat."

Farhad is about to respond to that but Mia doesn't give him the chance. "This wasn't about charity. You think I don't know your family can afford to replace the stuff those guys took? And this wasn't about some white girls making themselves feel good. This was about trying to let you know that there are people who really care about you, that for every jerk out there, there's somebody who thinks you're special, who's totally glad to have you for a friend and wants you to know that. At least until now. You can throw the jacket in the garbage too for all I care. And then you can go around looking sad or mad all the time. Just don't bother trying to do it around me anymore. Because I won't be there."

Mia turns and marches off so fast she's almost running. Her voice broke a little in that last sentence and I've never seen her that angry in my life. I'm trying to decide whether I should go after her or not but I don't. Instead I just sit on the bench wishing the last fifteen minutes hadn't happened.

A couple of minutes go by. Silent minutes. Finally Farhad sits down beside me. "I guess I kind of screwed that up." His voice is small and quiet, a major contrast from the yelling of a few minutes before.

"Maybe," I say, not wanting to overstate it.

"She called me an asshat."

I nod. "She did."

"Wow, I've never seen her like that."

"Me neither."

"Asshat."

"It could have been worse," I point out. "She could have used a different second syllable that also starts with h."

He looks at me and after a few seconds a small smile appears. "Yeah, you're right. So what do I do now? I don't think she's going to just-let-it-go-and-we're-good."

"No, I don't think that's going to happen."

"I should probably apologize."

"Might be a good idea. But only if you're actually sorry."

"I *am* sorry, Dom. Ever since the break-in at the pharmacy, this whole thing has been driving me crazy.

I know I've been a jerk to be around. I've been a jerk to you too. And I'm sorry for that."

"The biggest thing is we all want to help and we don't know how."

"Yeah, I get that. I've got really good friends and I know that too. Seriously." He pulls out his phone. "Now for the hard part."

He starts typing like crazy. It looks like he's going to be a while so I pull my totally beat-up copy of *Moby Dick* out of my backpack. I figure I might as well knock off a chapter or so since I'm about three chapters behind the rest of the class, thanks to all the evenings I put in memorizing my lines for *Wait Until Dark* instead of reading. I'm about four or five pages along when Farhad slaps me on the shoulder and says, "You gotta see this, man. This is genius."

He hands me his phone and I read.

> *Hey Mia*
>
> *How ya doin'? Actually I know how you're doin'. You're mad. Pretty smart of me to figure that out, huh? Yeah, I picked up on that because of the name you called me which I will not repeat because as you know I am not a person who ever uses what*

my little sister calls "swears." No sir, you won't hear any swears out of me. Anyway, I am writing this to tell you that you were right to be pissed (oops, I mean upset) at me. I know I've been hard to be around. The worst part is when I've been all mad and grumpy and depressed, I know I'm doing it but I can't seem to stop myself. Then I feel even crappier afterwards, especially when I'm that way to you and Dom who is sitting beside me right now pretending to be reading a book for English. But what I want to say is that I am honestly sorry. I can't promise I won't get down and bitchy (is that a swear?) ever again. But I really am sorry and I really am going to try to be more like I used to be before ... you know. Oh, yeah, and thanks for the jacket and the trainers as well as the photocopies of Danielle Hamilton's notes."

I look up at him, not understanding that part.

He nods. "Yeah, they also photocopied Danielle Hamilton's notes for me. Danielle Hamilton has the best notes in the school; I'm gonna be a damn genius."

"Yeah." I go back to the phone.

All of that was an amazing thing to do and I totally appreciate it. I got my trainers out of the garbage— those are tough shoes they weren't even scuffed. Anyway I know this is sort of long so if you skipped ahead to the last line, I'll just say again thank you and I am so sorry. I love having you for a friend.

Your favourite Asshat

Farhad

"What do you think?"

"Might be the worst apology letter ever." I hand him his phone.

"That's kind of what I was thinking."

"But it might work."

He nods and grins. "That's kind of what I was thinking."

"Only one way to find out."

He looks down at his phone, hesitates for a few seconds, then hits send.

After that, it's weird. He just sits there staring at his phone, willing it to ping.

"You might have to be a little patient here," I tell him. "She might not get it right away. Maybe she doesn't

David A. Poulsen

have her phone with her. She could be taking a shower or something."

He doesn't answer or look up so I go back to Moby Dick. It's probably ten minutes before his phone pings and he looks up at me like he's afraid to read it.

"Go ahead, man, I know you're dying to see what she said."

He reads for a few seconds, then looks up, his eyes clouded and serious. He shakes his head, then suddenly jumps up, yells, "Yeah!" about as loud as I've ever heard him yell and he high-fives me.

"I take it you got good news."

He holds up his phone, clears his throat and reads.

> *Farhad*
> *I love you and forgive you. But you are*
> *still an asshat, not my favourite asshat—*
> *just an asshat.*

"And then she put a bunch of x's and o's. I bet you don't get x's and o's. That's kisses and hugs, you know."

"Yes, I do know that and no I don't get x's and o's but she's also never called me an asshat."

He high-fives me again. And it feels like Farhad, the

old Farhad, the *real* Farhad is back. At least for now.

The only dark side of this whole sunny picture is that I know there are still some people out there who are consumed with hate. And they aren't likely to go away anytime soon.

16

MAY 24

_____

Take Me Out to the Ball Game

It's been almost three weeks of more or less peace and quiet. Mia and Farhad are friends again. There have been no more incidents involving Farhad or his family either at school or at the pharmacy. And no new developments in the investigation of the murder at 624 Edmund Avenue, at least none that the police have made public.

The Satin Wagon has been behaving itself. School's been okay although it seems like the workload has been ratcheted up with exams getting closer.

Which brings me to baseball. I am sitting in the dugout by myself after our third game of the season. So let me recap. In the first two games, I went 6 for 9 including two doubles, one with the bases loaded. In the field I made a couple of pretty nice catches in left field and threw out a runner at home who was trying to score from second on a single.

Game three of our season ended maybe a half-hour ago. The one big difference with this game was that Callie was here, seeing me play for the first time. I went 0 for 4, struck out twice and booted an easy play in left that resulted in a run for the other guys—the hated Marlins who, by the way, beat us 8–2. The only good part was that Callie had to leave right after the game which meant I didn't have to face her. Instead I am alone in the dugout, thinking I should re-title this chapter "Take Me out *of* the Ball Game." But I've been feeling sorry myself long enough that I'm thinking it's time to move.

My cellphone rings and I look down at it. Callie. I spend a few seconds deciding whether to take the call or run out into the street and throw myself under a bus. I answer it.

"Hey, yeah, I know I sucked and—"

"Where are you?" She sounds out of breath like she's been running and she also sounds like there's something wrong.

"I'm still at the ballpark. Are you okay?"

"No, no I'm not okay. Can you come and get me?" She recites an address—somewhere downtown.

"Yeah, I'll be right there." She's already ended the call so I grab my ball glove and run for the car.

I've been careful not to speed or break any other rules of the road since I got my license but I have to admit I break a few getting to where Callie is. I know the place or at least I know the camera shop across the street; I bought Mom a camera for Christmas there once. So I don't have to waste a bunch of time on Google Maps. The whole way there my heart is pounding and my mind is working overtime imagining all kinds of bad crap that could be happening.

I get there in maybe ten minutes. I run my tires up against the curb as I pull to a stop. The building is an old red-brick four-story place that was maybe a factory at one time but it's been fixed up and has offices and some of those cool loft apartments. But I'm not interested in any of that right now. All I want is to see Callie and find out what's going on.

I leave the car running and the driver's-side door open as I run for the front doors of the building. When I get there, the doors are locked and I spend several seconds shaking the doors and yelling Callie's name. But no one comes to the door. I see an intercom set-up to the right of the doors and I race over there and start pushing buttons and yelling "Let me in!" Which is stupid because, first of all, who's going to open the door to some guy yelling into the intercom and secondly, what do I do when I get in there? I have no idea where to start looking for Callie.

I punch the metal plate of the intercom and step back, frustrated and desperate to do something but not knowing what I *should* do. That's when I hear a voice, *Callie's* voice, not much louder than a whisper.

"Dom ... Dom."

That's all, just my name twice. It's coming from my right and I look over there. There are some bushes and small trees running along the front of the building and Callie steps out from between two of the bushes. She doesn't say anything, just looks at me and for a second I don't know if she's hurt. But one thing I know instantly is that something has happened. She's rattled and this isn't a girl who rattles easily.

I run to her and she folds herself into my arms, like she's trying to make herself small. But she only stays there for a second, then she steps back and is looking around.

I look around too but see nothing that doesn't look normal. "What's going on? What happened?"

"Let's get out of here," she says and she's dragging me toward the Satin Wagon, but her head is still on a swivel as she looks this way, then that.

She doesn't say anything else until we're in the car.

"Drive, just drive," she says.

I drive. Not as fast as I was driving to get there but pretty fast. Callie is looking behind us.

"Do you think anybody's following us?"

I look in my rearview mirror, don't see any headlights, not even a long way back.

"Nobody back there," I assure her. "You want to tell me what's going on?"

"I will," she nods. "I promise. In a few minutes. Let's just get away from here, okay?" And as she looks back again I can see she's not convinced we're not being followed.

I've read a few thrillers so I have a pretty good idea how to evade a tail if there is one. Or at least I know how they do it in books. A few lane changes, three right turns in a row, then one more right and back on the same road; I even cruise three blocks with my lights off. Finally I'm one hundred percent sure we're not being followed.

"We're okay now," I assure her.

Callie begins to relax and is not looking around anymore. But she also isn't saying anything. I ease up on my evasive driving and finally pull up in front of East Lake Park, a small but cool green space with a playground that my mom and dad used to take me to when I was a little kid.

Tonight it just feels safe. Lots of streetlamps, some families out walking and half a dozen kids playing what looks like dodgeball in one well-lit corner of the park.

"Come on," I say and we get out of the car and walk into the park.

I don't say anything more. I don't want to rush her but I reach over and take her hand. She offers me a partial smile and takes a deep breath.

"Sorry for all the drama," she says as we sit on something that looks sort of like monkey bars.

I shake my head and start to answer but she lifts her other hand to stop me.

She looks at me. "I didn't tell you the truth before, at least not the whole truth. About what happened that night."

She stops, releases my hand and turns to face me.

"When Mom and I heard the shots upstairs, like I said, we didn't know they were shots but we figured two loud bangs like that weren't a good thing. But I told you we stayed in my room until we were sure everyone was gone. That part isn't true. We waited maybe ten or fifteen minutes; then I couldn't stand it anymore. Mom stayed in my room but I didn't. Mom didn't want me to go up there and I know now I shouldn't have, but I couldn't stand just hiding downstairs while God-knows-what was happening one floor above us."

"Are you saying you went upstairs?"

She nods and bites her lip.

"Damn." I'm not sure what else to say. I don't want to tell her I think that was a really bad idea but I also don't want her to think I'm cool with her risking her life. "Damn" seems to about cover it.

"I know it seems crazy now when I think about it but I just couldn't stay down there any longer wondering if someone was about to break down the door and kill us both or if they were setting fire to the house or something. I had to find out what was happening. Besides we hadn't heard anything for a while and I figured maybe everyone had gone. So I snuck up the stairs and just when I got to the top of the stairs I saw a guy going out the front door."

She stops talking and looks at her hands, *our* hands. After a minute or so, she starts again. Mom doesn't even know this part ... and you can't tell her."

I nod. "Okay."

"I didn't know the guy. I'd never seen him before in my life. He was big, husky; he was wearing a leather jacket and a sort of grey toque; I'm pretty sure there was blood on the jacket. He had a bushy black beard. That's about all I remember about him. But when he got to the door, he turned and looked back into the house."

"Did he see you?"

"I don't know. I think he was looking toward where I was but I'm not sure about that. I've thought about it a lot. If he was the killer and he knew I'd seen him, wouldn't he have just come back and ..."

She stops again, shakes her head like she's trying to get rid of a bad memory.

"What about your dad? Where was he?"

"I don't know. I didn't see him, just the bearded guy."

"Did you tell this to the cops?"

She shakes her head.

"Why not?"

A small shrug. "I don't know; maybe the same reason I didn't tell you. I guess I was thinking the fewer people know about it, the less chance the killer—if he was the killer—would need to come after me."

It's not very logical thinking but I get it. Maybe I'd have thought the same way if I'd been the one who saw the guy going out the door.

"So what did you do?"

She pauses before answering. "Nothing. At least not right then. I think I was in shock or something. I just stood there for a while, I don't know how long, a few minutes maybe, and then I went back down to my room where Mom was. We came back upstairs a few minutes later and that's when we saw Dad packing up to leave and after that the ... body."

"And you're telling me this now because you think you saw the bearded guy tonight."

"Not think, Dom. I saw him. *I saw him.*" She practically shouts it.

"What is that place where I picked you up anyway?"

She shrugs. "I don't know. It's where I was told to go."

"Told? Who told you?"

"You remember I told you about the two Krebs brothers that lived with us?"

"Yeah. One of them was the guy who got shot."

She nods. "Right. That was Shane. Anyway, the third brother, the younger one, his name is Cal. And I saw him tonight. I came out of the ballpark to go to my yoga class and there he was, like he was waiting for me. He told me he had some information about my dad, something *I really need to know*—that's how he put it. Then he told me he was in this big hurry and didn't have time to talk right then and that I should meet him later at the address where you found me. But when I got there I didn't see Cal anywhere. I called his name a few times—nothing. So I figured I might as well give up and leave and suddenly that creepy guy, the guy I saw the night of the shooting came around the side of the building. At first he was in the shadows and I couldn't see him very well. I thought it was Cal. But then he came into the light more and I knew who it was. Same grey toque. Same black beard. He was carrying something in his hand. I don't know for sure if it was a gun or not but it might have been. Or maybe it was something he was going to hit me with. I don't know."

She stops again. She's been talking really fast through that last part.

"I've got part of a bottle of water in the Satin Wagon," I tell her. "You want me to get it for you?"

She shakes her head. "I don't know what he would have done if a car hadn't come down the street right then. Anyway he ran around the side of the building so they wouldn't see him. Dom, I was so stupid. It's like I was frozen there. But finally I decided to at least hide and I got down in those bushes where you found me. After the car went by he came back around the house. He stopped for a few seconds and he was looking around. I was sure he'd see me.

"I even closed my eyes because I was afraid they might give me away. But then he ran around hollering, calling me, yelling that he just needed to talk to me. I think he must have figured I ran off because he went racing down the street like he thought I'd gone that way and he could catch me. I didn't move ... I *couldn't* move. I don't know how long I stayed there. I was getting really cold but I was scared to come out. That's when I called you."

It's quiet now in the park. The kids playing dodgeball have left and there's almost no one there except us. I look at her for a long minute. "Okay," I say, "two things. First of all, promise me you won't ever do something like that again—go off on your own like that. From now on you call me first, okay?"

She shakes her head. "I don't need a protector, Dom."

"I know that," I say, nodding my head. "But there are times, like tonight, when it's just better if there are two of us ... you know?"

"Maybe." She gives me a small smile. "You said *two* things."

"You have to talk to the police. There's a dangerous guy out there who thinks you're a witness to a murder he committed."

The smile disappears and she shakes her head. "I didn't see him shoot Shane. What if he wasn't the killer?"

"Doesn't matter. You said yourself the guy's dangerous and I don't think he wanted to see you tonight to catch up on old times .... Whoa."

"What?"

"What if he knows you've moved back into your old house?"

"If he knew that, why would he have wanted me to meet him somewhere else; he could just come to the

David A. Poulsen

house and ..." She stops in mid-sentence, not wanting to finish the thought.

"Okay, maybe he doesn't know that now, but he could find out. He's obviously looking for you."

"I guess."

"Yeah, I guess too. So will you let the police know what happened tonight?"

"Okay, I will. Now could you do me a favour? Could you just put your arms around me and hold me for a while?"

I do and we sit like that for a long time, the stillness of the night surrounding us. I drop her off a half-hour later but when I get home I have a lot of trouble sleeping. I've got pictures of Callie and a guy I've never seen going through my head. The guy is big and has a beard and a gun. When I finally fall asleep I dream I'm crashing through these thick, prickly bushes looking for something or someone. I keep hearing whoever or whatever it is I'm looking for but I'm not seeing anything but bushes. And then finally there's a hand sticking out through one of the bushes. There's something in the hand but I can't tell what it is. I just know it's something bad and it's intended to hurt me. That's when I wake up all sweaty and with the covers tangled around me. I don't get back to sleep for a long time.

17

The Younger Brother

I'm a fairly serious student. Which isn't necessarily the same as being an outstanding student—I'm not, but I do take school seriously and (most of the time) do my best.

That said, I have to admit that all of the stuff going on in my life—my first car, my first real girlfriend, the start of baseball season, my best friend's challenges with unidentified racists—oh and my first involvement in a murder—all of it is starting to take a toll on my grades. They aren't a disaster, at least not yet, but Mia's prediction that I might end up going to City College when (and if) I graduate from high school ... well, I'm starting to think she might be right.

The good thing is the next time Callie came to one of my baseball games, I went two for four with a double and a three-run homer and we beat the dastardly Miller County Red Sox 6–5. A major pizza celebration followed and Callie and I performed The Lumineers "Ho Hey," and I have to say we weren't bad, especially on all the "hey's" and "ho's."

There's been no more bad stuff from whoever the guy is who was looking for Callie, but I still lie awake a lot of nights worrying about that, which is cutting into my sleep and is definitely not helping with those grades I mentioned earlier.

So I've decided I have to work harder at school. Which is why I'm back at school after baseball practice because I forgot my social studies text and there's an exam tomorrow. I'm not too worried about it because it's on the Renaissance unit. I've really liked this part of the course and I think I'm reasonably ready for the exam. But there are a couple of things I'd like to check up on, so I pull up in front of the school hoping one of the teachers is working late or maybe the caretaker is still around.

I park right in front of the front doors and let the Satin Wagon run while I run up the steps with my fingers crossed. Bingo, the doors are still open and as soon as I open the door I know why. I can hear basketballs pounding the floor in the gym which is just off to my left. Team practice.

I hustle down the hall in the direction of my locker; I don't want to leave the Satin Wagon out in front of the school for too long ... so down the hall to the far end, left turn, then a right and ... whoa.

I just start around the last corner to the hall outside our home room and good ol' locker number 926. But as I turn the corner I see a couple of guys at a locker just down from mine. Except I don't recognize these guys. I'm not sure why but right away my radar is doing what radar does and I don't like what I'm seeing. Luckily I get stopped quickly enough to duck back around the corner without their seeing me. And they're concentrating on whatever it is they're doing—and they're making some noise—so they don't hear me. I ease my way along the wall and sneak a peek around the corner.

And that's when it hits me. They're at Farhad's locker. I can't get a real good look at their faces but neither of them is Farhad. So now I have a decision to make. Do I take a run at the two guys and see how tough I am? Or do I just play it cool and see if maybe I can find out something—like who they are, do they go to this school, have they got some buddies waiting for them?

I decide to go with plan B. Partly because I don't like the idea of getting my head kicked in if I'm not as tough as I need to be. And partly because finding out something about these guys might do more good in the long run.

Except now I have another decision to make. What's the best way to execute plan B? If they just walk out of the school, it's going to be kind of hard to follow them on foot. And if they have a car, I'm pretty much hooped. So I decide to slip back out to the Satin Wagon and move to where I can watch the student parking lot. If they get in a car, I can maybe follow them and at least get a license number. And if they're on foot, then following them should be a piece of cake.

I get to the Satin Wagon, turn it around and park across the street from the entrance to the parking lot. From here I can see the parking lot—there's maybe twenty cars still in it and if I look in my rearview mirror I can see the front doors of the school if they exit that way.

And I wait.

It's maybe ten minutes before I see anything. Then the two guys come out of the school's south doors—the ones that lead to the parking lot. They're laughing and fist-bumping but I can't hear what they're saying—too far away for that but perfect for giving me a good look at them. And as I thought earlier, I don't know them. One of them, the bigger dude with his ball cap on backwards with something written on it—I can't make out what it is—looks a little familiar like I might have seen him around the school, maybe in the halls when we're changing classes.

They jog-trot across the parking lot and bail into a pickup. They hang a U-ey and are heading my way in a hurry. I duck down but it's not necessary; as I risk a peek over the edge of the window, I can see they aren't paying a whole of attention to anything but themselves—lots of laughing and they've got the radio cranked up full volume for some country song I don't know. They go by too fast for me to get the license number but I get a good look at the truck—a black Dodge three-quarter ton with a scrape on the right rear fender.

I decide it's futile to try to chase them. I'd have a heck of a time keeping up and if I did they'd probably figure out I'm following them. I'm sure I'll recognize the truck when I see it again anyway. But that's not

David A. Poulsen

my biggest takeaway from the afternoon's excitement. It turns out there's a third person in the pickup—the driver—and it's someone I recognize—actually know quite well. The guy at the wheel of the pickup is Foster MacLennan.

Here's my problem. I have some information but I'm not sure what exactly I should do with it. In fact, I'm not all that sure that what I've got, or what I think I've got, is all that big a deal. Sure I saw two guys doing something to Farhad's locker—I'll know in the morning what that was—and I saw them jump in a pickup with another guy and take off. But the only one of the three guys I actually know wasn't one of the two guys at the locker.

The obvious answer is to do what I was instructed to do—what the whole school was instructed to do—take what I saw to the cops or at least to Mr. Turley. So Foster MacLennan gets hauled into the office, says he doesn't know anything about anybody breaking into a locker and who knows, maybe he says he was the only one in the truck and then it's his word against mine. And even if Mr. Turley and the cops believe me, what are they going to do?

I curse myself for not thinking to take out my phone and get some video of what was going on at Farhad's locker. Because the truth is I haven't got much that's useful. At least not yet.

I head back to the school and this time I arrive just as the custodian Mr. Jenks is locking the front door. He glares at me but he's not all that serious; Mr. Jenks is everybody's friend. He pushes open the door and sets his hands on his hips and says, "Okay, Dominic, what did you forget?"

Mr. Jenks is one of the few people in my world who calls me Dominic. I'm not even sure how he knows my name but he does.

"Something for a test tomorrow. Do you think I could go get it? I'll hurry, honest."

"Yeah, yeah." I can see he's trying not to grin. "But you know that rule about no running in the halls?"

I nod.

"Well, that rule doesn't apply after five o'clock so get moving."

I get moving.

I'm at top speed heading down the hall partly because I don't want to hold Mr. Jenks up any longer than I have to and partly because I want to take a quick look at Farhad's locker to see if I can figure out what the two guys were up to. I round the corner, race to my locker, and have the book I need out of there in about four seconds. I close my locker, snap the lock shut and look around. If Mr. Jenks is coming down the hall to see how I'm doing, I won't be able to stop off at Farhad's locker.

But I don't hear any footsteps so I move down the ten lockers or so to Farhad's number 914. I check out the door but I don't see anything. There's no lock—they must have cut it to break in and then tossed it—so I can open the door. Again just a quick look. And other than the standard mess that is usually the inside of Farhad's locker, I don't see anything. There's a smell that's not quite right—probably what's left of a week-old lunch—but I'm not seeing anything. There's a pile of books and papers on the floor and I start to reach in to look under them when Mr. Jenks's voice booms down the hall.

"Dominic, I'm locking the door in ten seconds."

I slam the door shut and turn on the jets back to the front door. I can see Mr. Jenks has the door open and I'm thinking it would be cool to just keep running out the door and yell thanks to him as I go by. Mr. Jenks would think that's pretty funny. But at the last second I think of something and skid to a stop, panting and grinning.

"Thanks again," I say. "Uh ... can I ask you something?"

"If it means staying in the school for more than five more seconds, the answer's no."

"About fifteen minutes ago, a couple of guys went out the parking lot doors," I point in that direction which is totally unnecessary; Mr. Jenks knows where the parking lot doors are. "Did you happen to see them?"

"I saw a couple of people heading in that direction. I didn't see if they went out that exit or not."

"You don't happen to know them do you?"

"I know one kid's first name, that's it."

I bob my head up and down, then lie through my teeth. "I sort of know them too, but I just can't remember their names."

"Well, the one kid is Cal something-or-other. That's all I can tell you."

18

MAY 31

The Locker

Mia and Farhad are already at the bench basking in the morning sun when I get there but I'm a little later than usual because I cruised the school parking lot for a couple of minutes looking for a black Dodge three-quarter ton with a scrape on the passenger side rear fender. No luck.

But I figured it was early and lots of students hadn't arrived at school yet. I finally gave up, parked the Satin Wagon and made my way to the bench. A couple of heys and hugs later, I sit in the space between them and look from one to the other.

"Okay, this morning's question of the day—how common a name is Cal?"

They think for a minute, then Mia says, "Well, there's Cal—gary." She giggles.

Farhad reaches across me to give her a high-five, then says, "And Cal—ifornia."

"Ha ha, you guys are hilarious. I'm serious. How many Cals do you know?"

They try to get the dumb grins off their faces, not all that successfully, and finally Mia shrugs, "I'm not sure I've ever actually met anybody named Cal."

Farhad says, "Maybe it's short for something, you know like Dom and Dominic."

"Okay," I say, "good point. I don't know ... maybe Calvin."

"Or how about Callie?" Farhad is grinning again.

I have to admit until this exact moment I hadn't made the connection—Cal and Callie. Okay, that has to be a coincidence. Weird, but a coincidence just the same.

"So the bottom line here is there probably aren't a lot of Cals in the world."

Mia shakes her head. "Why are we having this conversation?"

I stand up. "You're right. Farhad, I think we should go to your locker."

"What?"

"Your locker, we need to go there right now."

"Are you on something this morning, Dude? First the Cal thing and now—"

I interrupt him. "No, although I admit I probably sound like it. But just go with me on this, okay? Let's go to your locker."

I don't want him going there by himself. Not today. I'm still convinced that even though I hadn't seen it, the two mystery men I'd seen the day before had been up to something. Finally he rolls his eyes and the three of us head up the concrete steps and into the school.

Mr. Turley's standing outside the office smiling and waving at everybody as we head down the hall. As we're going by, he says, "Hey guys, I was addicted to the hokey pokey but I turned myself around."

We groan in unison and Mr. Turley laughs and yells, "Have a great day!"

Mia isn't in the same home room as Farhad and me and she turns left at the library with a "See you guys later."

As soon as she's gone, Farhad stops me. "Okay, what's going on? Why are *we* going to my locker when *we* have never gone to my locker together before?"

"Okay, here's the thing. I came back to school last night about five o'clock to get a book I needed for an

The Dark Won't Wait

193

exam. I saw a couple of guys at your locker. I couldn't tell what they were doing but I don't imagine it was good. Then I saw them leave the parking lot in a pickup. I didn't know them. I figured if they wrote some crap in your locker or something I didn't want you to be by yourself when you saw it."

I'm not sure why I didn't tell Farhad about Foster MacLennan right then, but I guess maybe I didn't want him starting a fight in the halls or doing something even crazier.

I can see Farhad's anger building. "Okay, let's find out what today's surprise is going to be."

As we start walking again, I decide to see if I can lighten the mood. "After they left I took a quick peek but I didn't see anything. One piece of advice, my friend, don't leave an old lunch in your locker for more than a day. Not a real sweet smell."

He looks at me. "I've never left lunch or any food in my locker. Never."

I'm trying to think of what I should say next but we're at the locker.

He looks at it for a minute without opening the door.

"Lock's gone," he says.

"Yeah."

He opens the door and we both take a step back. The smell is way worse than it was the night before.

We both look and can't see anything, no graffiti, no gross pictures, or whatever it is that's making the smell.

"I know that smell," Farhad says. "It's something dead."

I'm guessing he's probably right and I'm also guessing that whatever's in there is under the pile of papers and stuff at the bottom of the locker.

He starts to reach into the locker but I grab his arm.

"I don't know if I'd do that, man; it could be something toxic."

He shakes his arm free, reaches in and pulls out all the papers that are on the floor. It's all I can do to keep from barfing.

The cat is on its back. There's a fair amount of mostly dried blood around its neck and face and I figure they had to have cut its throat. Tied around what was left of its neck is one of those cheery little cards people put on bouquets of flowers and stuff. I can read the message from where I'm standing.

"Hey, you could be next. Have a nice day." And there's a smiley face. A smiley face with whiskers.

Farhad looks like somebody who's been punched in the stomach. Hard.

I'm trying to think of something to say but the truth is I've got nothing, at least nothing that can make even a little bit of a difference as we look at the horror that's in Farhad's locker.

He turns to me. "What do you know about this?" It's not an accusation, just a demand for information.

"Just what I told you. I saw two guys, guys I don't know, at your locker last night. I couldn't see what they were doing and then I saw them later in the parking lot. I asked Mr. Jenks if he saw anybody in the school last night and he said he saw a couple of guys and one of their names was Cal but he didn't know the kid's last name."

"Cal," Farhad repeats the name, drawing it out, thinking about it.

"Problem is we don't know for sure that the two guys *he* saw are the same two guys *I* saw," I tell him. "We need to know that before we do anything stupid to somebody just because his name is Cal."

"Cal." He says it again and I realize he didn't hear any of what I just said. He looks down again, then bends down, shakes his head and says, "Shit."

"What?"

"This cat. It's Bernie."

"Bernie."

He stands up and looks at me. "Bernie. It's our neighbour's cat. There's a little girl there, Priscilla, she's maybe five. This is her cat. She loves Bernie. I saw her lots of times carrying that cat around, sitting on the porch with him on her lap, feeding him—this is really sick, Dom."

"We need to talk to Turley."

"What's he going to do? He going to get Priscilla's cat back to her without its throat cut? He going to—"

I hold up my hand to stop him. "I don't know what he can do. Or what the police can do. But I know one thing. Turley needs to know about this."

I'm ready to argue more if I need to but a couple of other students, a couple of niner girls, stop and look at the mess in the locker.

"Omigod!" The first one practically screams it.

The second girl doesn't say anything but she's headed for the washroom in a hurry and I'm pretty sure I know what's going to happen when she gets there. Her friend looks at Farhad, then me and heads off, also in the direction of the washroom.

I step ahead and close the locker door.

"Turley," I say again.

Farhad nods once and we turn and start for the office.

19

LATER, JUNE 1

Deception

We've spent two hours, first with Mr. Turley, then with the same two police officers who were here for the assembly. I've told them all that I know (except for the Foster MacLennan part—I'm still not sure why I've kept that to myself but I have, at least so far).

The two officers are getting ready to wrap up our meeting. Staff Sergeant Wheeler closes up his notebook and looks at Farhad and me. "Okay, thanks for this, guys. I know this is tough, especially for you, Farhad, but I want to repeat a couple of things we talked about at the assembly. No vigilante stuff. I don't want you two out there trying to be the Hardy Boys. Leave the investigating to us. I know it must feel like it's taking forever. But we'll get the people who are doing this—

trust me. And the other thing is let's keep the details to ourselves for now—especially names. We don't know who Cal is or that he actually had something to do with putting that cat in the locker. Until we know more, and we *will* know more, let's not get a bunch of people blaming someone who might not be to blame."

I listen and nod. But so far it seems to me the police haven't got very far. I know they're working at it, probably working hard, but I'm thinking they might need a little help. I almost laughed at the Hardy Boys reference—I loved the Hardy Boys when I was younger, but I also get that what happens in books isn't always real or believable. And this isn't a Hardy Boys book. This is real life with real bad guys doing horrible things to cats and to people they don't like.

And one of those people is my best friend. Because of that I don't intend to back off. I'll have to be careful, I know that, but I'm thinking there might be some things I can do that will help to make this nightmare go away.

And it starts with a guy named Cal.

———————

I wasn't very focused in class the rest of the day. Farhad's dad picked him up right after school to help at the drugstore and Mia had an audition somewhere so I'm sitting on the bench by myself right now trying to map out a plan. I'm trying to think like an investigator, but the truth is I don't actually know how to do that. This much I do know: all I've got is a name. Cal. I don't even know for sure that he's a student at Hastings although it seems like a good bet since Mr. Jenks knew his name.

But hey, it can't be that difficult to get an answer to that question. So back into the school, this time to the office. Mrs. Steeves is at her computer tapping away at the keys. I glance toward Mr. Turley's office. The door is open and he's not in there. I'm glad about that since he was there when the Staff Sergeant warned us about trying to play detective. Which is pretty much what I'm doing.

"Hey, Mrs. Steeves, how was your day?"

She looks up. "Oh, hi, Dom. My day has been very good, thanks. How about you?"

"Oh yeah, mine was good too."

There's a pause while I try to think of how to get where I'm going.

"What can I do for you, Dom?"

"Uh ... so I found a textbook ... out in the parking lot ... and it has the name Cal inside the cover but that's all. I was ... uh ... wondering if you could tell me the kid's last name so I could get it back to him."

"Oh, you can leave it here in the office and we'll make sure he gets it." She looks up at me and smiles like she's expecting me to pass it over the counter to her.

"Oh ... uh ... yeah, I could do that all right. But it's out in my car and I ... uh ... just kind of wanted to get it back to him myself, you know."

She's still smiling. "Well, aren't you the boy scout. Okay, just hang on."

She taps keys for a minute or so and then she writes something on a pad of paper next to her computer. Then she tears off the top sheet of paper and passes it to me. "Two Cals and a Carl," she says. "I threw in the Carl just in case.

"There's Calvin Mayhew in 9F. And there's a Cal, just Cal, last name Krebs, that's with a K; he's in 11D. And Carl is in 12B ... Carl Honeycutt. What textbook is it, Dom?"

"What ... oh ... uh ... chemistry, yeah, chemistry. I don't know what grade."

"Well, if it's chemistry, that rules out Calvin Mayhew. It's just science in Grade 9; then chemistry and physics start in Grade 10."

"Right, that narrows it down for sure. Hey, thanks a lot Mrs. Steeves." I'm starting to feel really crappy about lying to her, especially when she's trying so hard to be helpful. I just want to end the conversation and get out of there.

I turn and start for the door. But I don't make it. Mr. Turley walks in. Ten seconds—that's all I needed.

"Hey, Dom. What's up? You wanting to see me?"

"No, Mr. Turley, just had a question that Mrs. Steeves helped me out with. Have a great evening, sir."

"Sure, Dom, you too."

I escape but I know that if Mr. Turley asks Mrs. Steeves what my question was, I'm toast. He knows that a kid named Cal was leaving the school not long after the dead cat was put in Farhad's locker. And now here's me asking about a kid named Cal. After being warned more than once about trying to be a private detective.

But I can't think about that right now. I just learned that the youngest of the Krebs brothers—the jerk who tried to set up Callie with the guy she saw leaving the house after the shooting—might also be in on the stuff that's been happening to Farhad.

My head is spinning. Is there some connection between the two totally different crimes? Or does little brother Krebs just happen to be a racist creep in addition to all the other great things about the Krebs family?

Sorry, Mr. Turley, I'm going to have to spend a little more time in private detective mode. Once I know a little more, maybe then it will be time to give what I know to our school principal and the cops. Right now, all I've got are some vague suspicions, a couple of hunches and next to no evidence. Or maybe I'm just trying to justify my decision not to play by Mr. Turley's rules.

I've already made up my mind what I'm going to do. I'm thinking the time has come for me to do a little surveillance. I need to find out where Cal Krebs lives and then follow him and see what I can learn. Of course, there's a problem. The problem is the Satin Wagon. It's just a little too obvious, especially since I've been driving around in it pretty well nonstop since Mom gave me the car. A lot of people have seen it and a lot of people have seen me *in* it. Meaning that it's going to be crystal clear to anybody with even a few brain cells when he looks in

David A. Poulsen

the rearview mirror and sees the world's most famous 1981 Plymouth Reliant Station Wagon back there that he's being followed and who is doing the following.

And my bike is kind of out of the question—might be just a tad slow. So I've got two problems. I decide to go old school to try to solve the first one—where Cal lives. First I try the phone book. Only one Krebs in the book—Jacqueline Krebs. Didn't Callie say the youngest Krebs lived with his mom? Or did she say stepmom which would mean the last name wasn't likely Krebs. One way to find out. I pull out my cell phone and call the number in the book. A woman answers after three rings.

"Hi." I use my most cheerful voice hoping to sound somewhere between teenager and telemarketer. "Is this Jacqueline Krebs?"

"Who's calling?"

Okay, not the response I was expecting.

"Uh ... this is ..." I look around in a panic. I need a name. I spot a Tim Horton's across the street. "This is ... Tom Horton calling. Actually, I was calling for Cal if he's around." Now trying to sound like Cal's oldest and best friend. Then it occurs to me—what if this is Cal's house and what if he's at home and he comes to the phone?

"There's no Cal here."

"Right, well, okay then ... guess I have the wrong number. Sorry to bother you." I end the call and punch myself in the head. *Tom Horton?*

Okay, on to Plan B. Which would be so much easier if I *had* a Plan B. The phone book idea didn't work. So what now? I'm still thinking surveillance in the Satin Wagon isn't going to work. I have to work out a way I can follow Cal from school to wherever he lives; then once I know that, I set up my little spy operation. All I need is a set of slightly less obvious wheels in which to do my following and spying.

And then just as desperation is setting in, Plan B hits me right between the eyes. I need to trade vehicles with Mom for a couple of days. Thing is, I can't tell her the truth, that I need her car to carry out a little detective work. I'm pretty sure Mom will be in the Mr. Turley camp on that score. *Leave it to the police to do the policing.*

So that means lying to Mom which I hate doing. But I really don't see that I have a choice. All I have to do is think of a really believable reason for us to switch cars.

I'm still working on that problem when I get home.

David A. Poulsen

Mom is already there and there's a very nice smell coming from the kitchen. A very nice *meat loaf* smell.

Mom's got the tunes on the stereo and she's singing along to some song that I'm sure was huge in 1995. Singing *and* meat loaf.

"Hey, Mom."

"Hey, Sweetie, how was your day?"

"It was okay but why do I have this feeling that yours might have been better? You seem to be in a pretty good mood."

"You know, you might be right. The sale of the Swendon place will do that for you."

"Whoa, that's awesome." We high-five in celebration.

The Swendon house is a listing Mom's had for several months. And unlike a lot of the very average bungalows Mom usually lists, this place is pretty upscale. Which means it probably sold for a large slice of cash. Which means a nice commission for Mom. And that is what has brought about meatloaf (one of my all-time favourite meals) and the old-time rock and roll on the stereo.

But my Hall of Fame evening is just getting started. Sometimes good old-fashioned luck beats a solid Plan B by a mile.

"Dom, there is one thing I wanted to talk to you about."

"Sure, shoot."

"I was wondering if it might be possible for me to borrow the station wagon. Remember I told you a while back that our firm is moving to a larger office a couple of blocks from where we are now?"

I hate to admit it but I don't remember her telling me that. Probably because I wasn't listening.

"Sure," I say.

"Anyway, the move is this week, and I've got a ton of boxes and files and stuff to get to the new office. It would only be for a couple of days. And I'm sure you'll do fine in the Lexus. It really has quite a nice stereo."

It's all I can do to keep from dancing around the room screaming, "I win, I win!"

Instead I work very hard at keeping a straight face and say, "Hey, Mom, if it helps you out, I'm happy to trade cars. Of course, hordes of beautiful women will be totally heartbroken when they rush up to the Satin Wagon and discover I'm not the one in the driver's seat."

"I'm sure the hordes and I will somehow get through it."

"I've got a game tonight." I glance at my watch. "I'm

gonna have to go right after hitting the meatloaf, but I can get my gear out of the Satin Wagon when I get back to give you more room for your office stuff."

She kisses me on the cheek. "I can't make the game tonight but go hit something more than meat loaf, okay?"

"Will do."

——————————

And that's it. Twenty-two hours later I'm sitting in the Lexus in the back row of the parking lot, the black pickup with the scratched fender in sight a couple of rows away. I've got the shades on and a Colorado Avalanche ball cap pulled down low. On the seat beside me are binoculars, a thermos of coffee and two meat loaf sandwiches I made from last night's leftovers. I even brought a yellow notepad and a couple of pens and my phone is ready to snap some pix if there's anything I think I should photograph.

School ended a few minutes ago and I raced out here so I'd be ready when the black pickup moves out.

I'm in a terrific mood. Turns out I kept my promise to Mom the night before. Two line drives, as a matter of fact, a pair of doubles, one with runners on second and third. We beat a team we were tied with in the standings—the Southside Steamers—7–4. Callie was at the game but had to leave after the fifth inning for her Yoga class. But she was there when I picked up the two RBI's with the rocket to right centre in the bottom of the third.

She texted me a few minutes ago but I didn't read the text. I don't want to have to lie to her if she asks me what I'm doing.

A couple of guys have just piled into the black pickup. I'm too far away to see if one or both of them were the guys at Farhad's locker. I try the binoculars but there are too many vehicles in the way. Doesn't matter. What's important right now is to follow that truck and see if I can get a line on where Cal Krebs lives. And I'm betting Cal Krebs is one of the people in that truck.

And that's when I almost have a heart attack. The passenger door of the Lexus is jerked open and, before I can react, someone leaps into the front seat.

It's Farhad.

"What the hell are you ... you nearly ended my life right there. What's up anyway? I've got an appointment and I have to—"

"Cut the BS. I know exactly what you're doing. You think you're the only guy who can figure some things out. I know you're about to follow that black pickup and I'm pretty sure I know why but we don't have time to go into it right now because they're leaving."

I look over at the pickup. Farhad's right—they're moving.

I look over at Farhad. "Listen, I don't think you—"

He cuts me off. "Are we following those guys or not?"

I pull the Lexus into drive and work my way around the outer perimeter of the parking lot making sure there are cars between the pickup and me. Farhad is leaning over with his elbows on his knees concentrating like he's a gunner in a World War II bomber. I was a little worried that there'd be tons of people all leaving at the same time and I could lose the pickup and its occupants before I ... make that we ... even got started. But so far there's just a few cars separating us. Perfect.

The pickup turns left leaving the parking lot. I get a break in traffic almost right away and am able to make the left turn with two SUVs and another pickup, this one red, between me and the guys we're tailing.

What follows is fifteen minutes of mind-numbing

boredom. My first attempt at being a private investigator is a long way from a CSI episode. The highlight is when the black pickup pulls into a 7–Eleven and the driver jumps out and runs inside. I'm not totally sure but I think it might be Foster MacLennan.

"Drive by, drive by!" Farhad barks at me.

"I know how to tail somebody!" I bark back.

I drive on by. Actually, Farhad's right again—I'm pretty sure that's what the detectives in the novels do. A little way past the 7–Eleven, I pull over to the curb. I did manage a glance over as I rolled past the pickup and the guy riding shotgun and staring down at his phone looks a lot like one of the guys I saw at Farhad's locker.

"The guy driving—that looks like MacLennan."

"Uh-huh. But he wasn't one of the guys at your locker. I'm positive about that."

"But he hangs out with creeps."

"Looks like it."

Farhad, who was careful *not* to look over at the pickup, says, "And the other guy. You think that's Krebs?"

"I think so."

I'm looking in my rear-view mirror. The pickup is

still parked. Then it hits me. I swing around to look at Farhad. "How did you know Cal's last name was Krebs?"

"Did a little detective work."

"I hope your detective work didn't involve Mrs. Steeves. If Turley figures out we're doing a Batman/Robin impersonation ..."

He shakes his head. "Actually, it was elementary, Watson. I got out last year's yearbook, spent maybe three-quarters of an hour scanning pages of photos and bingo, got a last name. I asked a few people in the lunchroom today if they knew Cal Krebs and a kid I knew in Grade 11 pointed him out for me. He's even uglier than his yearbook photo and that's not easy to do. Anyway, after school I followed him out to the parking lot to see if I could learn anything interesting and guess who I see is hot on the trail."

"Yeah," I say.

I check the mirror again. No movement from the pickup.

"By the way," Farhad says, "who's who?"

"What?"

"Batman and Robin. Which one of us is Batman?"

I shrug. "I don't know."

"I do," he says. "I'm Batman."

I chuckle because I think he's kidding around.

He shakes his head. "It's not a joke. I don't need some white guy saving me or trying to right the wrong that was done to me and my family. That's my job. You can help and I appreciate it but I'm serious, Dom ... I'm not your deputy and I'm not your sidekick. I'm Batman."

I think about telling him he's been watching too many westerns but I realize this isn't the time for lame one-liners. The weird thing is I totally get what Farhad is saying. I agree with it and I like it. I *was* trying to be some white savior. Like he couldn't look after himself. Here I am thinking I'm the anti-racist and actually I'm being totally racist. Not on purpose but that doesn't matter.

I'm about to tell Farhad what I was just thinking but I'm not sure exactly how to say it. Instead I hold out a fist and he bumps it.

"Batman," I say.

He nods.

"So the two guys in the truck are Foster and Cal," he says. "Interesting combination."

I check the rearview mirror again and this time they're moving. When they go by us a couple of minutes later, I make sure I've got my head down and facing away from the road, like I'm talking on my phone or texting. Farhad's scrunched down too. We give them a minute to get a little further ahead before I pull back into traffic.

I wish I could say that first night of surveillance was productive or even a little exciting. It was neither. A few minutes later they pull onto a side street in a pretty upscale neighbourhood and the pickup eases to the burb. I pull over half a block back. Foster MacLennan hops out and heads up the sidewalk toward an expensive-looking house. There's a sweet-looking Escalade in the driveway. The guy I think is Krebs runs around to the driver's side of the pickup and jumps in.

I turn to Farhad. "Which is it, surveillance on MacLennan or follow Krebs?"

He points at the pickup and I nod, pull out and fall in behind the black truck. This time it's off to the exact opposite part of town. A dumpy house on a dumpy street. My mom sells the odd "fixer upper." The place is more of a burner downer. Krebs pulls the pickup onto a weed-infested driveway alongside a small house that I'm guessing was last painted to celebrate the end of World War I.

This time I park three-quarters of a block back. I check that my phone camera is on and ready and hand Farhad the binoculars. We're all set to make a move.

———————————

Except we don't make a move because Cal doesn't make a move. All night. Nobody comes; nobody goes. I tell Farhad that if this is Cal Krebs, he's the little brother of the guy who was murdered at Callie's house and that the two brothers were heavy into the drug scene.

"Solid citizens," he says.

From then on we talk about football, Farhad's favourite sport; baseball, *my* favourite sport; Farhad's latest crush—there are about two of those a week—and where we think we'll live when we get through school and university. Farhad says New York and I say in whatever city drafts me for their major league team. Farhad doesn't laugh at that. Instead he says, "That dream can come true, you know."

Pretty cool thing for him to say. We eat the sandwiches and drink the coffee. The most exciting part of the evening is trying to figure out a bathroom strategy, especially after the coffee. That's something those crime novels never talk about. About nine o'clock things get pretty desperate and I go for a short stroll and find what I hope is a secluded spot in a nearby alley. Apparently Farhad has better bladder control than I do; the only time he gets out of the Lexus is to stretch a couple of times.

We decide to be at least a little productive, so I recap what we know and Farhad writes it on the yellow note-pad. It's not a lot but some of it was news to Farhad. This is what Farhad wrote ...

> Shane Krebs was murdered at 624 Edmund Avenue. Callie saw somebody, maybe the killer, leaving the house after the murder. The killer (if that's what he is) saw her as well. Then some weeks later, the third Krebs brother sets up a bogus meeting for Callie where she sees the guy we think is the murderer. Luckily he didn't see her and she came out of that unscathed. So why would the brother of the murder victim be helping out the guy who shot his brother?

Then there's the whole other thing—the vandalizing of

my dad's drugstore and the stuff at my locker which we're sure involved Cal Krebs. Is there a connection between the two crimes? And where does Foster MacLennan fit into all of this?

So that's it. What we come up with is a lot of questions and not many answers. I'd hoped that tailing Cal Krebs might lead to some of those answers but so far ... notta.

It's now 10:30 and we decide it's time to shut down. The only positive that came out of the evening was a text from Mom to tell me the car switch would need to go on for one more day.

I drop Farhad off at his place and I drive home with one thought pounding through my brain like a Drake lyric.

Surveillance sucks ... surveillance sucks ... surveillance ...

More Detecting

The great thing about a bad day is that it doesn't take a whole lot for the next one to be better.

The next one *is* better. I'm flying solo this time; Farhad has to work at the pharmacy. But what makes this day a good day is that the tailing of the guy I was pretty sure was Cal Krebs is a little more interesting. He doesn't have anyone with him as he drives out of the school lot this time. And he turns right instead of left. Once again I leave three or four cars between us and try as much as possible to stay out of the lane Krebs is in so I'm not as easily visible in his rear-view mirror.

Longer drive this time. Two stops. The first is a convenience store. He's in and out in a hurry and has a package of cigarettes in his hand as he exits the store.

He stops, opens the package and lights one. Stands there for a minute smoking and looking around. Looks my way but I'm tucked in behind a motorhome half a block away and he doesn't spend a whole lot of time looking in my direction. He turns the other way, takes a few more drags on the cigarette, then gets back in the pickup and we're off again.

Once we're back in traffic he moves into the right-hand lane so I move over to the centre lane. Then he makes a quick turn into the parking lot of a strip mall. Once again I roll on by, turn right at the next corner and circle the block ... slowly and carefully to make sure I don't accidentally come face to face with the guy. I park the Lexus, throw the binoculars in a backpack, ease my way out of the car and cross the street away from the mall. I decide to kind of circle around, being extra cautious since I don't know what he's doing or where exactly he's going.

There's a tow truck, the only vehicle parked on the side of the street I'm on, so I move in behind it and pull out the binoculars. I adjust them to my eyes and by looking over the top of the tow truck's deck, I get a pretty good look at the mall parking lot. And unless somebody

David A. Poulsen

happened to be looking right at the tow truck with binoculars of their own, it's not likely they'd see me.

At first, I think Krebs has gone into one of the stores but then I spot him leaning against an SUV. He's got another cigarette going and he's talking to whoever's in the driver's seat but I can't see who it is. Actually, what Krebs is mostly doing is listening and nodding.

Then the passenger door opens and somebody I don't know gets out of the SUV. Krebs throws the cigarette down, grinds it under his boot. The two of them head off on foot toward a Chinese café and for a minute I'm thinking this is going to be another nothing surveillance where all I learn is that "the subject" smokes and likes moo goo gai pan.

Except they don't go into the café. They walk right by it and into a pharmacy that sits next to the café. I remember my phone and pull it out, ready. They're in there at least five minutes but finally they come out. The guy with Krebs is carrying a paper bag that looks like maybe it has the drugstore's name and logo on it. Hard to say even with the binoculars but that's my guess. It's a fairly big bag and it looks pretty full. If they're picking up a prescription for somebody, that person must have a hell of a lot wrong to need as many pills or whatever's in that bag. But maybe it's shaving supplies or something.

I grab my phone and get a couple of pictures of Krebs and the other guy face-on as they're coming back to their vehicles. And very quickly, the guy with the prescription bag gets back in the SUV, and Krebs climbs back in his pickup.

The SUV is coming right toward me. One of the entrance/exits to the strip mall is right opposite the tow truck. I duck behind the cab as the SUV turns right out of the parking lot and heads down the street. I sneak a look around the tow truck and see that Krebs is taking a different exit onto the road. I drop my phone in my backpack, turn and run for the Lexus, to continue my tailing of the guy. I just get the door of the car open and am ready to jump inside when something hits me. Hard.

No, make that someone. With a bodycheck that knocks the backpack out of my hands and drives my head into the side of the Lexus. Hard enough that I'm stunned for a minute. Whoever hit me pulls me around and slams me back against the car.

I'm looking into the face of Foster MacLennan. He's

got a good chunk of my shirt balled up in one hand and his other forearm is under my chin and pressing hard on my throat. I try to move but I'm a little dazed from the first hit plus MacLennan is bigger and I'm finding out quite a bit stronger than me.

His face is about fifteen centimetres from mine. His teeth are clenched and for a minute I figure he's going to hit me. I'm having a tough enough time breathing and trying to keep from choking. He eases off just enough to keep me from passing out.

"You dumb, dumb, dumb son of a bitch," he hisses at me. "Do you know who you're screwing with here? If those guys find out you're playing private-eye games and following them around, they'll shoot your ass and bury you where nobody will ever find you. Are you listening to me? You know how dumb you are? While you were following them, I was following you. And you didn't even know it. Hell, I saw you and your just-as-dumbass friend yesterday and I knew exactly what you were up to. You're just lucky it was me that saw you and not one of them. Where is he by the way?"

"Where's who?"

MacLennan presses harder with the arm he has

against my throat. It's getting hard to breathe, and I'm thinking I might pass out.

"How about you don't act like you think I'm stupid. You know who I'm talking about. Where is he?"

I'm having trouble talking but I manage to get out, "Busy today."

I manage to swallow but when I speak again it's more of a soft growl than anything. "What are you to those guys? Are you part of all the shit they're—"

He tightens the grip again. Still tighter and his forearm feels like it might crush my vocal cords and whatever else is in a person's throat. And again I can feel myself falling toward unconsciousness, but he pulls back just enough that I can hear and understand his words.

"I won't be warning you again. Leave this alone or you're gonna end up with more trouble than you could ever imagine. You were a dumbass fake cop in the play and you're an even dumber ass now. Except in this play, the dead people don't come back to life when the lights go on."

He pushes away and I slump to my knees on the pavement. MacLennan heads off up the street and I spend a couple of minutes trying to get some air into

David A. Poulsen

my lungs and massaging my throat to try to get it feeling like it's working again.

Finally I get my feet under me and I'm able to stand although I'm pretty wobbly. I know I've got a bottle of water in the car but it takes me a couple of minutes to actually get the door open and reach inside. I gulp some water and end up sputtering and coughing. The only good thing is that nobody has come along while I've been trying to recover from Foster MacLennan's attack.

A couple more minutes and I'm starting to feel like maybe I'm going to live. I drink some more water, this time without the coughing fit. I start to work my way around the car to the driver's side. I'm about to climb inside when I remember the backpack. The backpack with the binoculars and my phone inside. I stumble back around to the passenger side of the Lexus and at first I don't see it.

Panic is about to set in but I glance down again and there it is. It got knocked under the car while I was being … uh … warned not to keep doing what I was doing. I gather up the backpack, climb in behind the steering wheel and spend a long minute looking in my rear-view mirror.

I text Farhad to let him know the results of today's undercover mission. I tell him about Krebs's stop at the pharmacy and how Krebs and some guy I've never seen before come out of the drugstore with a bag full of who-knows-what. I don't tell Farhad about my encounter with Foster MacLennan, partly because I'm embarrassed that I got my ass kicked and partly because I don't want to listen to Farhad's bad jokes about it for the next year or so.

The thing that really pisses me off is that Foster MacLennan was right. I was dumb. I had no idea he was back there tailing me while I was tailing Cal Krebs. Which means that I have to be a lot more careful in the future. Because one thing I know for sure. This is a long way from over. And I'm a long way from done.

Pharmaceuticals, Part One

It was a few days before I could talk without sounding like I'd just had my tonsils out. So, a lot of texting. Callie wanted to come over and see if I was okay but I told her the doctor said what I had might be contagious. I didn't want her to see the bruising around my throat.

Last night's baseball game was not a lot of fun. I was still hurting, and swallowing wasn't my best skill. Running the bases was tough but since I managed only one infield single, I didn't have to do a lot of running. I wore a throat warmer and told our manager I had a bug and the doctor said I should wear it.

I was sick of listening to myself lying to people who didn't deserve to be lied to but I couldn't quite bring myself to tell anyone exactly what had happened. I saw

Foster MacLennan in the hall today between classes. Neither of us said anything but he looked at me the way I looked at the Satin Wagon when the carburetor wasn't working. It was like he was threatening me with his eyes.

I stared back at him, hoping that my face was saying, *You don't scare me.* The weird part is that even though he whipped me pretty good, I'm not really afraid of him. Although I have to admit I am taking his warning seriously. If I'm going to try to find out more about murders and racist vandalism and other criminal activity I'd better be a lot smarter about it than I've been so far.

Mom and I swapped back our cars this morning and it was good to be back in the Satin Wagon. I gave Mia and Farhad rides to school and told them I wouldn't be at the bench after school because I had some errands to run. Actually I have just one errand—to see Callie, partly because I was missing her after not seeing her for a few days and partly so I could show her the pictures I'd taken at the strip mall.

We exchange texts and I pick her up at her place. She's at the curb waiting for me and ten minutes later we're sitting in a booth at Vinnie's.

"Something I want you to see," I tell her.

"Wow, not even a *How was your day, I really missed you*?"

"Sorry, it's just kind of important." I show her the pictures on my phone. "You know those guys?"

"Sure. The older one's Jackie Krebs and that's the youngest brother, Cal."

I'm glad to hear that the guy I've been following actually *is* Cal Krebs. The second guy's identity makes sense. They're brothers for starters and neither one is exactly a solid citizen so no real surprise that they would meet up. I'm guessing they were probably up to something sketchy but I realize I don't have any proof of that.

Callie stares at my phone screen. "Where did you get these?"

"I took them at a strip mall. They went into a pharmacy; then they came out a little while later and left."

"Wait, you just *happened* to see them at that mall? Or did you follow them to that mall?"

"Uh, yeah, I guess I might have followed them. Or at least I was following Cal and he met Jackie there."

"Are you crazy? The Krebs family—those are really bad people. Are you trying to get yourself killed?"

"Callie, I'm totally sure that Cal was one of the guys who vandalized Farhad's locker. Which means there's a real good chance they also vandalized the Shirvanis' drugstore."

"Even if that's true, you need to go to the police before you ..." She stops in mid-sentence and looks again at the photo of the two brothers. "What did you say they did at the mall?"

"They went into that pharmacy—you can see it in the background." I point. "Right there."

"And you said Farhad's dad also owns a pharmacy, right?"

"Yeah, and ... whoa, wait a minute. You think there's some connection?"

She's still looking at the picture on my phone.

"I don't know," she says slowly. "The Krebs brothers and my dad are drug dealers. And now here's one of them going into a pharmacy, also known as a *drug*store. I just wonder ..."

"You think there might be some link between their drug dealing and their ... uh ... interest in pharmacies?"

She thinks for a minute, then shrugs. "If there is I can't think what it might be. It just seems like an odd coincidence that there are two pharmacies sort of involved with these guys."

I shake my head. "I don't know. People go to pharmacies all the time, for everything from cold meds to magazines to hair products. Maybe they were just getting some meds or something the day I saw them, but I kind of doubt it. And if it was them who did all the damage at the Shirvanis' pharmacy I'm still betting it was racial—a hate crime. It sounds like the stuff they wrote on the walls was just racist crap. And the same with Farhad's locker. It's all about, *Hey, you people who don't look and talk and act exactly like we do, we want you to go back where you came from.* That kind of garbage."

Callie nods. "You're probably right. So what are you going to do now?"

"I don't know. Mr. Turley, he's the principal at Hastings, has said we should go to him or the police if we see something that might be offside. I guess I'd just like to have something a little more definite than a bunch of my own suspicions before I do that.'

"I guess I can see that." She draws out the word *guess* to make it sound like she really doesn't see it. "But you can't forget that these are dangerous people. I know the Krebs brothers and they scared me every time I was around them. I don't want you out there trying to do something heroic and getting yourself beat up ... or worse."

"Got it, Boss." I grin at her.

"I'm serious."

"I know and believe me I'm not any more excited about me getting beat up than you are."

"Or worse," she repeats.

I nod. "Or worse."

She takes hold of my hands. "I'm not trying to be a pain in the butt. I just don't want anything bad to happen to you."

"Trust me, I'm in total agreement with you on that."

"Promise me you won't do anything stupid."

"Define stupid," I say.

"I'm serious. Promise me."

"Okay, I promise."

22

Pharmaceuticals, Part Two

I drop Callie off and start for home. But I don't get far before I pull the Satin Wagon to the side of the road. I need to think about a couple of things and figure I better not be doing that thinking while navigating traffic.

I'm sitting next to a house with a Private Sale sign in the front yard. Normally I'd make a note of the number and pass it on to Mom. Sometimes a call from a friendly, honest realtor like my mom will convince the person trying to sell privately to list the property with that friendly, honest realtor, aka Mom.

But this time my mind is working on other things ... like what Callie said about the two drugstores and how they might be related somehow to what's going on. She might be right. Or at least it's worth conducting a little research. I'm pretty sure research doesn't qualify as "doing anything stupid."

I call Farhad and relay Callie's idea. At first he doesn't say anything, then, "Hey, let me call you back; there's something I need to do."

He doesn't wait for my answer and is gone. I put my phone in my pocket and wonder how long I'll have to wait for Farhad to get back to me. Turns out it's not long. Like maybe two minutes.

"I talked to my dad about the thing with pharmacies and he's convinced the attack on our business was totally racially motivated. But he did tell me that a couple of guys came around and were talking to him about some deal on prescription drugs. My dad said it smelled fishy to him and he told the two guys to screw off."

"Wow, interesting. Did he say anything else about the two guys—what they looked like, what else they said?"

"Yeah, that's the thing. Dad didn't think it meant anything at the time and he still doesn't but he remembers one of them saying something like, "Bad decision, old man. You will regret this."

"So, a threat," I say.

"Sounds like it to me."

"Which makes Callie's theory all the more worthy of our attention."

"I was thinking the same thing," Farhad says. "So let's say the Krebs boys try it out on a few pharmacies. Some cooperate because they're afraid not to and some, like my dad, don't. So we know what happens when you tell them to take a hike but I wonder how often our boys make their stops at the pharmacies that are cooperating."

"Good question."

Neither of us says anything for a while. Then Farhad breaks the silence. "So we know one pharmacy that the Krebs brothers might have working for them. What if we were to keep an eye on the place and wait for their next visit? What's the term for that—stakeout?"

"Which is another word for surveillance, which is another word for torture."

"So would you rather talk to Turley or the police and just stay out of it?"

"No," I answer a little louder than necessary. "I'd like to have a few more real answers before we do that. So surveillance it is. But this time you bring the sandwiches."

So twenty-four hours later our research has begun. It's 5:42 PM and the place closes in eighteen minutes. Dali Drugs. We've been parked in the mall parking lot for close to an hour watching the place.

"I say we go inside, take a look around," Farhad says.

"Agreed," I nod. "But I don't think we should both go in there. One of us should stay out here and be ready to text the other guy if they suddenly show up."

"Okay, I'll go inside," Farhad says.

"Okay," I say. "Whoa, wait a minute. They obviously know you and I doubt that they know me. Maybe it would be better if I went in."

I can see Farhad is reluctant.

"Hey, Buddy. I'm not trying to take over. I just figure—"

"Yeah, yeah, I know you're right. Get going, they're going to close soon. And keep your phone handy."

I climb out of the Satin Wagon, cross the parking lot and enter the store.

I've never been inside before; I've only seen it long distance—when the Krebs brothers came out of the place with Jackie carrying a paper bag from the store.

David A. Poulsen

I wander the aisles for a couple of minutes pretending to look for something in case I'm being watched by a closed-circuit camera. But what I'm doing is just looking the place over—what they call in some of the old movies, "casing the joint."

I don't really know what I'm looking for but mostly I just want to be familiar with the layout of the store. The prescription area is at the back and is separated from the rest of the store by a counter along the front and side perimeters. Behind the counter two people are working, a man and a woman, about the same age; the man is Middle Eastern in appearance. There are two wickets along the counter-front of the prescription area, one for placing orders and one for pickup. The aisles run at a ninety-degree angle away from that part of the store. There's only one other person working in the pharmacy; she's younger than the two druggists and is manning the front checkout counter. I grab some cold medication off one of the shelves and step to the prescription order wicket.

The male pharmacist looks like he's filling a prescription, pouring some kind of pills from a large container into one of those small pill containers, like the ones I've seen Mom bring home from the drugstore when one of us needs some kind of medication. The woman is doing something on a computer. She looks up, sees me and comes toward me, smiling.

"Something I can help you with?"

"Uh, yeah, I've been having a little trouble with my throat and I was wondering if this stuff would help."

She looks at the product and says, "It's not bad, but depending on what's wrong with your throat, there might be something better. Do you have any other cold symptoms?"

I shake my head. "No it's just my throat. It's kind of ... scratchy." That's not a lie. Courtesy of my encounter with Foster MacLennan, my throat is still very definitely scratchy.

She points at one of the shelves in the aisle directly behind me. "The red box there. Second shelf from the top. Might be more what you're looking for."

I thank her, put back the box I'm holding and take the smallest size of the product she has recommended. I navigate the aisles one more time and get a pretty good mental picture of the layout. Then I head to the counter at the front of the store to pay for my medication, add two Mars bars to my purchase and head out, satisfied that I learned what I wanted to.

When I get back to the Satin Wagon, I tell Farhad that I have a pretty good idea as to the layout of the place and where the prescription drugs are dispensed.

"That's it? You didn't solve the mystery? Clear the case?"

"Nope, but I did bring you one of these." I pass him one of the Mars bars.

He grins. "Well, I guess that will do ... for now."

———————

It's two hours later; I've washed the dinner dishes— well, I've arranged them in the dishwasher and hit the start button—and it's time to call Callie before I take a run at my homework.

"Hey, I've got an idea," I tell her. "It doesn't really qualify as a plan, at least not yet, but it's an idea and I'd like to share it with you."

"Is your car in running condition?"

"The Satin Wagon? Are you kidding me? Does a duck have ... feathers?"

"That's not how that expression goes."

"I'm trying to be PG here."

"Right. So why don't you get in your car and drive over here."

"Well, let me see. Callie ... homework. Homework ... Callie. I can't decide."

"I'll see you in fifteen minutes." She laughs as she says it.

"Right."

Actually, I make it in twelve, even with a couple of manoeuvres to make sure I'm not being followed. The incident with Foster MacLennan kind of spooked me. But I'm here—624 Edmund Avenue. I run up the stairs and stop for a last look around before ringing the bell. Truth is there are some bad people out there and at least one of them has an interest in seeing Callie. And not likely to make polite conversation. So, yeah I'm a little extra-cautious ... maybe even *over*-cautious. But I'm not seeing anyone or anything that looks suspicious.

I'll skip over the details of the first couple of minutes after I get there except to say that Callie is able to take a pair of distressed jeans, an old sweatshirt (NYPD) and what looks like tie-dye socks and look like she should be in a fashion magazine.

She pours us iced tea she made while I was on my way to her house and we sit on the couch. There's a plate of Dad's chocolate-covered oatmeal cookies on the table.

"Okay," she says. "Let's hear your idea that isn't quite a plan."

I take a drink of the iced tea and eyeball the cookies. "I told Farhad about what we talked about before, you know, what you said about the pharmacies and how there might be a connection."

"Right and you said you didn't think so," she says.

"I know but the more I thought about it the more it feels like maybe I'm wrong."

The look on her face tells me she isn't following me.

"Okay, you mentioned a connection," I say. "So what do all pharmacies have? Prescription drugs. And we know there's a market for them."

"Sure, but that's just it. They're *prescription* drugs. You don't just walk into a pharmacy, head over to the prescription counter and say, *Yeah, I'd like a bagful of oxycodone and fentanyl, please.* You need a prescription."

"Or maybe you don't. What if they threatened the pharmacies—we'll burn your store down if you don't give us what we want."

She thinks about that. "Interesting theory. But the problem is that's all it is."

"Not exactly. That's what happened at Shirvani's Pharmacy a few weeks before the place was vandalized."

"How do you know that?"

"Farhad talked to his dad. Mr. Shirvani said a couple of guys came into the store and wanted to make some kind of deal on prescription drugs. He threw them out and they threatened him, said he was making a big mistake and would pay for it."

She thinks for a minute before answering. "That's interesting but you still don't really have much. I'm sure the police would say there's not enough there to make an arrest."

"True, but I wonder if there's a way we could find out a little more."

"How are you going to do that without putting yourself in some kind of danger?"

"That's where my idea comes in. Except it's getting to be more like a plan now."

She sips her iced tea. "Okay, let's hear it."

"Okay, I saw the Krebs brothers going into that pharmacy last Thursday. Let's just say they're involved in

David A. Poulsen

something illegal. And if it has to do with getting drugs, then there's a pretty good chance it's not a one-off."

"Meaning?"

"Meaning, they could be going back to that same pharmacy on a regular basis to get whatever it is they're getting."

"O ... kay." She drags it out and makes it sound like a question.

"So we have someone there when they go for their next pickup and maybe we can find out what they're up to."

She's shaking her head before I even finish the sentence. "Look, in the first place, why are you doing this? You told me your principal said nobody should be trying to play detective and that's exactly what you're doing. And secondly, the Krebs brothers know me and they probably know you too, at least Cal does. Same goes for Farhad. So if they see one of us in that pharmacy, they're going to be very suspicious and I already told you these guys aren't people you want mad at you. You remember our conversation about not doing anything stupid."

"I remember."

"And you prom—"

I cut her off. "I get that and you're right. And actually,

I'm not sure Cal Krebs does know me. I didn't know him, hadn't even heard of the guy before all this stuff started happening. Anyway, it doesn't matter because none of us is going to be in that pharmacy when the brothers Krebs come around."

"Who then?"

"Actually, I have the perfect person. And she just happens be a talented actor. She'll have them believing she's just a shopper looking at shampoo or skin cream."

"And what if Krebs shows up and he's just buying something for his allergies or something?"

"Then we haven't lost anything, have we? And either way, whether we get some evidence I can take to Mr. Turley or not, this will be it for Dominic Cantrell, Private Investigator. Although that does have kind of a nice ring to it, don't you think?"

She shakes her head quite energetically.

"No, it doesn't."

"Anyway, I'm out of ideas."

"Good," she says. "Because your ideas are going to get you a stay in a hospital one of these days. And, for some reason, I'd miss you." She smiles at me for the first time in a while.

"Listen, Callie. I imagine you've already figured this out, but I'm the happiest guy in the world that we're together. And I don't want to do anything that might change that. But this is important. I want to do everything I can to help Farhad. He's the closest thing I've ever had to a best friend. Let's see if we can find any connection on this pharmacy thing and then, like I said, I'm out of it."

"Okay." Another smile. "Now you better get home and get at that homework you were telling me about." She leans over and her lips brush lightly against mine.

"Right. There is one other thing though."

The smile disappears. "What?"

"I was wondering if I could take a couple of those cookies with me."

She laughs and punches my arm. "Take them and get out of here."

I take three.

Pharmaceuticals, Part Three

Mia needed no persuasion at all. She was on board five seconds after I finished explaining to her what we wanted her to do. She even had some ideas of her own about how we might learn more about the Krebs brothers and what, if anything, they were up to in the pharmacy.

I thought about tailing Cal Krebs again, thinking it might be interesting to know if he and his brother went to other pharmacies. I suggested it to Farhad and he was opposed to the idea.

"Let's get one thing done before we take on something else," he said.

I had to admit he was probably right, especially after promising Callie that our little spy operation would be the last bit of detecting I would do.

It's taken two days. Mia, Farhad and I sat outside across from the strip mall yesterday (Thursday, one week to the day after the first sighting) for an hour and a half but the Krebs brothers didn't show up. For the first time I began to wonder if maybe my imagination was out of control and all of this was, in a word, silly.

But I convinced Mia to try it again the next day. "Hey, there's no guarantee they go on the same day every week," was my reasoning and she agreed, but I wasn't sure we'd get a third day out of her.

So here we are. It's 4:25 and I can feel Mia getting a little impatient. Farhad's been practising a comedy routine for some banquet he has to attend next month. Or maybe it's a wedding. I have to admit I wasn't really paying attention when he told us about it. Nerves, maybe.

He's actually pretty funny, no surprise there, but I'm not really in a laughing mood as we inch closer to closing time at Dali Drugs. We're in the Lexus. I convinced Mom I needed the "good car"—it killed me to say that—for an auto shop project where kids were supposed to practise making estimates of repairs that might be needed. When she asked me why I couldn't use the Satin Wagon, I told her it would be too hard for the kids in the class to find parts for a car that old. The whole story was crap and probably didn't even make sense but Mom, ever the good sport, went along with the idea. However, just as with Mia, I doubt I'll get another day out of the Lexus.

Suddenly, none of that matters. They're here. Mia is staring at her phone and doesn't even see them arrive.

"Hey." I poke her in the side harder than I meant to. "It's time for you to win an Academy Award. They're in that black pickup. Jackie's the one driving."

She sets her phone down and looks at the black Dodge.

"Okay, got it."

Farhad points to her phone. "Take that with you. If there's a problem, text one of us."

"And what would you do?"

It's a good question and I don't have a ready answer for it and neither does Farhad. So I say, "Just text me."

"Right." She drops the phone into the pouch of the hoodie she's wearing and hops out of the Lexus.

The Krebs brothers drive around looking for a parking spot which gives Mia time to get from the Lexus to Dali Drugs. I have the binoculars ready; Farhad has one of the school's video cameras. He managed to borrow it but I'm not sure why.

"Video footage of them going in and out of the place won't really mean much," I tell him. "It's what happens inside the pharmacy that matters."

He nods but is still gripping the video camera; maybe he's thinking there could be a shootout in the parking lot and he'll get exclusive footage for the six o'clock news. Our phones are on the seat. We watch Mia make her way through the parking lot and into the store. I've gone over the layout of the store with her, even drew her a map.

Watching her navigate the parking lot, I'm instantly worried because, of course, once she's inside, there is no visual contact; in fact, there's no contact of any kind. Unless she texts. And if she texts, that means something's wrong.

I have never hoped more *not* to receive a text from someone. And I have never been more nervous sitting in a car waiting for someone—oh wait, that's not true. There was that first time I met Callie, but this is a different kind of nervous.

This time, Jackie goes into the store by himself. Cal stays in the truck. He's not that far from us but once again I've got the sunglasses and the ball cap pulled down low. Farhad has my *Baseball Digest* magazine up in front of his face but he keeps looking around, over and even under it. It probably isn't necessary because it looks like Cal is staring at his phone. Probably playing a really stupid game. I'm also keeping an eye out for Foster MacLennan. I don't really need a repeat of his launching himself at me. I was extra careful on the drive over here and I'm pretty sure we weren't followed.

The minutes tick by. Slowly, very slowly. I figured Mia would be maybe two or three minutes, max, but we've been sitting for closer to ten. I look at Farhad; he looks at me.

"This is taking a long time," he says.

"Yeah, it is."

I look at my watch. Farhad checks his phone. "What if we missed her text?"

"We didn't miss her text," I tell him. But I'm just as nervous as he is. I stare at the pharmacy trying to will the door to open and Mia to come out. Still nothing and another couple of minutes tick agonizingly by.

Now I'm thinking maybe *I* should text *her*. Which I realize is a really dumb idea; it could blow her cover.

David A. Poulsen

That's when Jackie Krebs strolls out of the pharmacy. I train the binoculars on him and I can see he's carrying a paper bag almost identical to the one he had with him the last time he and his brother came out of that place. He walks straight to the truck, jerks the driver's side door open. He jumps in behind the wheel and a few seconds later they roll out of the parking lot and disappear in traffic.

I keep watching the door of the pharmacy waiting for Mia to appear. But there's still no sign of her. Another five minutes tick by and now I'm pretty well in full panic mode. Farhad gets out of the car, then gets back inside and a few seconds later gets out again.

My mind is racing through bad thoughts like nightmares on a bad night. What if Krebs figured out Mia was watching him and ... what if ... I mean, what if he shot her or something? What if she's dead in there? These guys have already been involved with one murder. I'm just about to say, "Let's go," when Mia pushes open the front door and ambles out of Dali Drugs, looking like this was the sort of thing she did every day.

She's even eating something that looks like a Kit Kat bar. And she's smiling. She gets to the car without actually making eye contact with either of us. Farhad gets out to let her in. She climbs in, settles herself and finally looks over at me.

"Well, that was interesting," she says.

"What kept you? We were getting worried out here."

"Well, I didn't just want to follow him out of there; that might have made him suspicious."

I look at her and realize she's right. I nod. "Okay, good call. You said it was interesting. *What* was interesting?"

"Yeah," Farhad says. "We need some details here. Did you see Jackie Krebs?"

She looks at Farhad, then at me like we're annoying little brothers. "Of course I saw Jackie Krebs. That's why I went in there."

"Oh," I say, a little snark in my voice. "I thought maybe you just wanted to get a Kit Kat bar."

She holds it out to me. "Like some?" I can see she's having a really good time.

I take a finger of Kit Kat and glare at her, craving information.

She chews, swallows and finally appears ready to talk. "When I saw Jackie Krebs come into the store, I worked my way into the aisle one away from the prescription

David A. Poulsen

counter. There was only one other person in the store and she was looking at vitamin supplements so she wasn't all that close to us. Jackie went straight to prescriptions. There were two people working there, probably the same ones that were there when you went into the store. As soon as Jackie got to the prescription order wicket, the woman turned away from what she was doing and went into a kind of office area and closed the door.

"What was weird, Jackie didn't say anything, at least not that I heard. But he had something in his hand, a piece of paper that looked kind of like a prescription. It was kind of hard to tell from where I was."

I groan. If Jackie had a prescription, maybe the whole thing is on the up-and-up and I've got nothing to show for our little spying operation. "Okay what happened next?"

"The guy working in prescriptions lifted up this hinged part of the counter and Jackie went right in there."

"You mean where all the drugs and stuff are?"

"That's not allowed," Farhad says.

Mia nods and I feel a whole lot better knowing that Jackie Krebs is not just a normal customer. Not if he was allowed in the back where all the drugs are kept.

She continues. "Then they went to the very back of the prescription area so I couldn't see them for a while. When they came back into view, Jackie was carrying a bag. It looked pretty full of something. Then he lifted the counter thingy and let himself out of there. He didn't even look back at the pharmacist and he said, 'I'll see you in a week.' And that was it. He just kept walking right out of the store. I could see the pharmacist and he just stood there watching Jackie leave. He looked really unhappy."

"And you could see all this good enough that you can tell Mr. Turley what you saw."

She smiles at me. "Better than that." She holds up her phone. "I've got the movie."

Once again I didn't even think about putting technology to work but thankfully Mia did. She taps a couple of buttons and passes the phone to me and I watch. It's all exactly as Mia described it except at the very end, after watching Jackie Krebs leave the store, the pharmacist opens a drawer and puts what looks like the prescription into the drawer. And just about at the same time, the woman pharmacist comes out of the office and the two of them look at each other. Neither is very happy and neither of them even moves for quite a while. They just stand there and if I had to describe how they looked I'd say crushed. The video ends.

I high-five Mia. The drugstore probably has closed-circuit cameras but who knows if they were working or looking at the right place at the right time. This way we've got what I hope is pretty good evidence that something is going on.

"That's good stuff," I tell her. "Weren't you worried about one of them seeing you videoing?"

She shakes her head. "I just stayed back in the aisle, ducked down and held my hand out with the camera. I was just hoping my aim was okay and I was getting what we needed."

"Your aim was perfect."

She chuckles.

"What's so funny?" Farhad asks.

"I didn't really pay attention to what was in the aisle where I was ducked down until after I shut my phone camera off."

"So what was it?"

"Condoms."

I look at Farhad and he looks at me. And for the next couple of minutes the car is filled with the sound of three teenagers laughing. In fact, we laugh so hard and so long that after a while my sides actually hurt.

It was worth it.

———————

It's Monday morning and the three of us are in Mr. Turley's office before school starts. He doesn't say anything until we finish telling our story. Farhad and I do most of the talking since we know more of the details and Mia takes him through the making of her pharmacy video although I notice she leaves out any mention of the condom aisle.

The other thing that doesn't get mentioned is Foster MacLennan, partly because I really don't know what his involvement is in all this and partly because I'm still not wanting to talk about getting my butt whipped.

Mr. Turley watches the video twice, then sits back in his chair and looks at us, first at Mia, then at Farhad, then at me. I can't say he's looking all that pleased, especially when he's looking at me.

Finally, he leans forward and rests his thick forearms on the desk. "You two don't take instructions very well, do you?"

David A. Poulsen

Two? I have a pretty good idea who he's not as mad at. He's cut Farhad some slack because of what he's been through.

Neither Mia nor I offer an answer.

"What you've been doing is both reckless and dangerous. And it's exactly the opposite of what you were told. Every student in this school was instructed, not once but at least a couple of times, that we didn't want you guys out there trying to be detectives. And you were also told, by both the police and by me, that if you did encounter something you thought might be worth looking into, you should bring your concerns to either your teachers or me or the police."

"Yes, sir," Mia says.

I jump in. "But isn't that what we're doing, Mr. Turley? And Farhad and I did come to you after the locker thing." I know it's weak even as I'm saying it, but I guess I'm not really wanting to get dumped on without offering some kind of defense.

Mr. Turley shakes his head. "And that's when you needed to back off and let the police do their work."

Right on cue, the same two officers who've been at the school a few times already, arrive at Mr. Turley's door. He'd called them earlier when I stopped by the office to tell him we might have some information that could be useful. He couldn't meet with us right then but told me to come back after first period and to bring Mia and Farhad with me.

After Mr. Turley's spiel, I figure we're really going to hear it from the cops but maybe they can tell from the looks on all our faces that we've already been read the riot act. Anyway they skip the lecture and have us take them through the whole thing again. I tell them that Jackie and Cal Krebs are the brothers of Shane Krebs who was murdered at 624 Edmund Avenue. I tell them what Callie told me—that they were part of a drug operation along with Callie's dad. I'm sure the officers already know all that, but I say it anyway because it leads to our guess that maybe there's something going on with pharmacies and possibly prescription drugs. I even throw in my theory that maybe that's the connection with Farhad's dad's pharmacy business and the vandalism of the store and even Farhad's locker. Farhad adds in the part about his dad being threatened by a couple of guys a few weeks before the attack on the store.

The officers don't say much but when we've finished

David A. Poulsen

telling them what we know or at least what we *think* we know, they pull out a paper for Mia to sign, sort of like a receipt for her phone which they take with them promising to return it once they've made a copy of the drugstore video. No questions, no yelling, not even any nasty looks. In fact, as she hands Mia the receipt, Constable McCartney smiles and says, "Thanks, guys." Once they're gone, Mr. Turley seems in a little better mood.

"I don't suppose I have to say it again," he says, but there's a little more of a smile in his eyes than there was before.

"No, sir." I figure I'm the one who should answer since I'm the one who's most guilty. "The Cantrell Detective Agency is officially closing its doors."

He smiles at that. "Listen, I hope you know that the police officers and I are concerned for your safety. These guys could be involved in some kind of major drug operation and maybe even a murder. That makes them dangerous people that you need to stay as far away from as you can." He pauses, and then the smile gets a little bigger. "But I have to tell you that you did a pretty darn good job here and what you've learned should be helpful. So, thank you. But that's it, okay.

Game over. New team on the field. Do you understand what I'm saying?"

"Yes, sir," I say. Mia and Farhad nod.

Mr. Turley's smile returns, bigger this time.

"It's too bad though ... the Cantrell Detective Agency. Catchy name."

24

JUNE 13

Good News - Bad News

We got word the next day that there had been some arrests. Although we weren't told the names of those in custody or even how many people had been arrested, Constable McCartney came by to thank us again for our help with the investigation. And she kind of hinted that the arrests involved people we had had previous contact with.

With the bad guys off the street, at least *some* of the bad guys, and with the school year winding down, I realize the old Farhad is finally back. And that's the best part. I know things are returning to normal because as we're sitting on the bench on a spectacular June Tuesday, he leans over toward me.

"Hey, Dom." He's talking in this loud stage whisper. "Those girls who just walked by … you know their names?"

I shake my head.

"Of course you don't," he grins. "That's because you're not me. They're Cindy Melaney and Deborah Wong, not *Deb*-or-ah Wong but De-*bor*-ah Wong. And both of those young ladies find me extremely attractive."

I roll my eyes and glance over at Mia who is wisely paying no attention to us and is rapid-fire tapping at her phone. I look back at Farhad.

"And you know this because?"

He taps his temple. "Experience, ol' buddy, something I realize you don't have. It's in their eyes."

"Their eyes," I repeat.

He points two fingers at his eyes. "It's right there, if you know what to look for. And if you hang out with me this summer, maybe I'll share some of my secrets to understanding the female psyche."

I'm saved from more of his chatter by the welcome music—Taylor Swift, who else?—but the whole time I'm shaking my head as we head into the school, inside I'm happy as hell to have my best friend back ... *all the way* back.

But a day that got off to such a promising start goes sideways in a big way right after school. We're back at the bench and this time it's Mia who's all bubbly. She's been offered a part in a summer production of *The Mean Girls*.

Farhad and I are both making all the appropriate noises to show her how happy we are for her when my phone pings. A text. From Callie.

> *Hey*
> *I need to see you.*
> *Can you make Vinnie's*
> *in half an hour?*

That's it. No x's and o's. Not even a *Love you, Callie* at the bottom. I text her back.

> *I'll be there.*
> *Are you okay?*

But I don't get an answer.

I look up and realize Mia and Farhad are both watching me. Maybe it's the look on my face but they both seem to sense there's something wrong.

"I gotta go." I glance at my watch. "But I can run you guys home first."

Mia shakes her head. "We'll walk. It's a gorgeous day. You go do what you have to do."

Farhad nods agreement. "You need any help, bro?"

I'm not sure how to answer that.

"I don't know. I don't think so, but ... something's ... I don't know, Callie ..."

I'm just blathering so I finally just shrug, give them both a little wave and start off in the direction of the student parking lot. I'm walking fast with my head down, trying to think of all the things that could make Callie send a text like the one I just got. Because that's not Callie; it just isn't. The big break-up? *It's not you, it's me. There's this other guy and ...*

That's about when I look up. Right into the face of Foster MacLennan. One thing I haven't been able to get my head around is if the Krebs Brothers are in jail or wherever guys like that go while they're waiting to go on trial, why is their buddy (and I'm pretty sure their accomplice) still around and going to school like nothing's happened? I'd love to have that conversation with him, but not right now.

He's leaning against the brick wall of the school, smoking a cigarette and looking like a character from *The Breakfast Club*, which is a really old movie my mom loves and to tell the truth, isn't too bad.

He nods at me and I sort of nod back at him. I get the feeling he wants to talk to me but I keep on walking and he doesn't say anything. I run the last fifty yards or so to The Satin Wagon and I'm at Vinnie's at least ten minutes ahead of the half-hour Callie mentioned in her text. I pick a booth and order a Coke from nosy Dakota. She actually smiles at me when she brings the Coke, and I smile back. No sense carrying a grudge ... I guess.

I haven't touched the Coke yet when Callie arrives and slides in across from me. I can see she's been crying. I reach across the table and take hold of both her hands.

"Hey, what's wrong? Are you okay?" Which is stupid because I can see she's not okay but I guess it's what you say at times like this.

She doesn't answer right away, just shakes her head and the tears start again. I get up to come around the table to sit beside her but she holds up her hand to stop me and I sit back down. I want to ask her again what's going on but I realize that would be a mistake. Whatever it is, she'll tell me when she's ready.

"I got home from school today and Mom was there." She says it slowly, careful to pronounce each syllable of each word like every one of them is painful. And important. I know that whatever she's about to tell me, it's not good.

"She came home early from work." Callie looks at me, I mean *really* looks at me for the first time since I sat down. "She wanted to have a talk with me. She had something really important she wanted to tell me."

She's not looking at me anymore. In fact, she's looking everywhere *but* at me. The table, our hands, my glass of Coke, the wall ... but not at me.

I open my mouth to say something but close it without making a sound. A long minute passes with neither of us speaking.

Then, "Dom ... we're moving away, Mom and me. We're going to Nanaimo. In British Columbia."

I release her hands, rub mine over my face, trying to process the words I just heard. "But you just moved back into the house. It doesn't make sense ... I mean ... why?"

"Mom said there's just been too many bad things happen here. She wants us to have a new start in a new place, new people ..."

"Did you try to talk to her, tell her she's wrong, that—"

"That's the thing, Dom. She's not wrong. I mean, think about it. My dad's a drug dealer; we don't even

David A. Poulsen

know where he is. Mom's job is okay but she doesn't love it. And she's not making enough money to make the mortgage payments without my dad helping. Oh, and there's that little thing about us living in a house where there was a murder ... a murder for God's sake! What part of that sounds like a great life?"

"But what about us?"

She looks again at me. "That's what I said when Mom told me we were moving. What about Dom and me? We ... we really care about each other. You know what she said to me? Dom just turned sixteen, you're only fifteen. I know this seems like the only love you'll ever know, but believe me—"

I hold up my hand. "Yeah, yeah, I know exactly what she said. It's the same thing my mom would say."

I pick up my Coke but set it down without taking a drink. Dakota arrives at our table, looks at Callie. "Can I get you something?"

Callie glances up at her and shakes her head. Dakota doesn't leave right away. Maybe she can see something's wrong.

"If you want something later, just let me know, okay?" She actually looks like she feels bad for Callie.

"Thanks," Callie says. Dakota leaves and I take Callie's hands again and we sit like that for a long time.

"When?"

She shrugs. "I guess once I finish my year at school and as soon as she can get the house sold."

The irony is, normally when I hear about a house about to hit the real estate market, I'm thinking I need to tell Mom, see if she can get the listing. This time that's the last thought in my head. In fact, I'm not sure what thoughts *are* in my head other than this is the worst day of my life and there is exactly *nothing* I can do to make it better.

Callie's voice is soft and sad. "I guess I won't be going to Hastings, after all. I was thinking it would have been so great for us to be at the same school."

I nod my head and look at her. "That would have been amazing." I wish there was something really profound I could say—the kind of stuff the guy always says in those movies. But this isn't a movie and I don't have the words.

Instead I say, "You want to do something tonight, maybe a movie or a pizza at Vinnie's or ..."

She shakes her head. "I'm sorry, Dom. I don't think

David A. Poulsen

I'd be very good company tonight. I think I just want to go home."

"Yeah, okay. I understand." Actually I don't. I want to be with her. There's nobody else I'd rather be with right now and the last thing I want is to be by myself. But I can see that her mind is made up.

She smiles at me. It's not a big smile but I'm thinking it's probably the best she can do right now. "There is one thing I'd like you to do for me."

"Name it."

"My birthday's coming up. Can we have a party?" She manages a smile and I realize, sixteen or not, just how much she means to me.

I nod, slowly at first but it builds as I think about it.

"You want a party? *You want a party?* It just so happens that I am one of the great party organizers on Planet Earth."

She shakes her head. "You don't have to organize it. I know it sounds crazy but I want to organize it myself. You just have to be there. And bring Farhad and Mia and if they want to bring somebody, that's cool. Just make sure you don't bring a date for yourself."

"I was kind of hoping I'd already have a date."

"Yeah, that's what I was hoping too."

25

The Party

I've come to realize there's a downside to working with the police. No matter how much information you give them they do not feel obligated to return the favour.

That meant that a week and a half after our chat in Mr. Turley's office I didn't know any more than I did then. They did finally tell us that the Krebs brothers were in custody—Cal in the Youth Detention Centre, Jackie in adult jail—and they were awaiting trial. Neither had been granted bail.

But what did that really mean? Were the Krebs brothers going to be off the streets for a long time? If so, what had they been charged with? Were Mia and I in danger for ratting them out? What about the mystery man Callie saw the night of the shooting? Were the police any closer to solving that case and capturing the shooter? And Callie's dad—what about him? Where was he? Was he alive or dead? They didn't seem to know anything or if they did, they weren't telling us.

Those were some of the more pressing questions that had been swirling around in my mind since we'd turned over the phone video Mia had shot in Dali Drugs. And that's why today is a very big deal as Farhad and Mia and I sit in Mr. Turley's office waiting for the two police officers to arrive. Again.

The thing is, before this year I had been to the office exactly twice—once to get a late slip and once to pick up the lunch my mom had dropped off after I'd forgotten it. And suddenly it's like I'm in the office every few days. They should give me a frequent-user bonus card.

And it seems like most of the time I'm in the office, the cops are there too. I'm pretty sure a lot of the kids at school must think I'm a serious lawbreaker. Farhad has started calling me Scarface—you know, from the movie about Al Capone.

Mr. Turley called the meeting and actually phoned us at home last night to request that we be in his office at I PM.

It's now 12:56 and no one has spoken since Mr. Turley came back into the office after getting the three of us bottled waters. I'm looking at my hands, mostly so I'm not looking at Mr. Turley. For some reason I'm really nervous. I mean what if none of what we've given them matters? What if none of it will actually be useful in putting Jackie and Cal Krebs away? What if the druggist at Dali Drugs refuses to say anything or has been scared off by some of the Krebs brothers' friends? Or, God forbid, what if they were actually just getting a couple of totally normal and legal prescriptions filled? If that was what we were about to hear, this would be a very dark day.

The waiting is over. Staff Sergeant Wheeler and Constable McCartney arrive, greet the three of us, then take the two vacant chairs Mr. Turley has set out for them.

"Seems like I'm spending as much time with you as I do with my own kids." Staff Sergeant Wheeler grins at me.

"I guess so, sir." I'm too nervous to return the grin. He hasn't joked around a whole lot in our previous meetings and I don't know if that's a good sign or a really bad sign.

The two officers and Mr. Turley do some small-talking for a minute or two but I don't really hear any of it. I glance over at Mia and Farhad. Both of them look a lot calmer than I feel.

Then Staff Sergeant Wheeler nods to Constable McCartney who looks at me. "We need you to tell us again how it came about that you and Farhad and Mia were at the Dali drugstore that day you videoed Jackie Krebs."

I'm tired of telling it but I nod and give it to them all again, from when I first saw the two guys at Farhad's locker and finding out that one of them was Cal Krebs, then following him, once to his house, then the second time to the strip mall where Dali Drugs was located. I tell them that the second trip to the pharmacy was kind of a hunch and that Farhad and I had convinced Mia to follow Jackie Krebs into the drugstore to see what he was up to.

"Actually videoing him in there, that was Mia's idea."

As I wrap up my story, the constable looks at her notes, then nods to her partner.

Staff Sergeant Wheeler looks at me. "We wanted to hear it from you again to make sure your story hadn't changed."

"Why would I change my story?"

"Sometimes as people have time to think about things, they remember something they left out before or maybe recall that the shirt they thought was blue was actually red. That can be a problem when we get to court."

"I remember it all pretty clearly."

"And you told us you didn't know the second guy at Farhad's locker."

"I didn't know either one of them at the time. It was later that I found out that one of them was Cal Krebs. I never did find out who the other kid was."

"Would you recognize him if you saw him again?"

I think about that. "Maybe. He was taller than Cal and kind of skinny. I mostly saw him from behind but a couple of times he turned so I could see him from the side. Then later when the pickup truck went by me on the street I got another look at him. It was quick but I think I might recognize him if I saw him again."

Constable McCartney pulls an envelope out of a briefcase-looking thing she's carrying. "I'm going to set out four photos on Mr. Turley's desk. The photos are numbered. If you see the boy you thought was with Cal

David A. Poulsen

Krebs that day at the locker I want you to tell me the number of that photo."

She lays the photos out and I stand up so I can bend over them to see better. It doesn't take long. I'm pretty sure one of the four is the guy I saw but I take my time and look at each photo a second time, just to be sure.

I sit back down. "Number three," I say.

"Are you sure photo number three is the person you saw with Cal Krebs at Farhad Shirvani's locker after school on May 28?"

"I'm not one hundred percent positive but I'm pretty sure that's him."

Staff Sergeant Wheeler leans forward, rests his elbows on his knees. "His name is Lenny Purvis. He's been living in the Krebs's basement for the past year or so. He's been in our system before but mostly for small stuff, shoplifting, a couple of break-and-enters. But it turns out Lenny didn't really like his previous encounters with juvenile law enforcement. So he was quite willing to tell us what he knew about the activities of the Krebs brothers. And he knew quite a lot. It was Lenny and Jackie and Cal Krebs who did the number on Shirvani's pharmacy."

Looks like I was wrong about the police sharing information.

"If he's confessed why would you need me to identify him?"

"Even with what he's told us, every piece of corroborating evidence is important if and when we get to court."

"So will I ... will we be testifying in court?"

The Staff Sergeant shakes his head. "We can't say for sure at this point. But let me continue for a minute with what we do know. Shirvani's was one of four pharmacies Krebs went to with a scheme to acquire restricted prescription drugs that could be sold on the street for pretty big money."

I shake my head. "I can't see Mr. Shirvani being willing to go along with something like that."

"He wasn't. None of them were. But Krebs threatened to torch their businesses if they didn't go along. Mr. Shirvani complied the first time they came in but he told them to get lost the next time Krebs walked into the store. Lenny Purvis told us that the two Krebs boys figured vandalizing the place was better than burning it to the ground, both as a warning to the other pharmacies and as a way to express their racist views about the Shirvani family."

I look at Farhad and I know what he's thinking. His dad didn't mention that he'd gone along with the Krebs's scheme the first time. I'm guessing that's a conversation Farhad and Mr. Shirvani will be having at some point.

Mia asks, "But why kill that poor cat and do that stuff to Farhad's locker? They'd already made their point."

Staff Sergeant Wheeler nods. "That was Cal and Lenny's deal—had nothing to do with the drug stuff. That was just a plain old hate crime, pure and simple."

There's silence in the room for a while as all of us try to get our heads around what we've just heard.

"One thing I don't understand," I say. "I didn't think people could just walk into a pharmacy and get those drugs. Aren't there controls that prevent that?"

The Staff Sergeant smiles at me. "You guys ask really good questions. The answer is yes, there are. There's something called the Triplicate Prescription Program— TPP. It's a type of prescription that has to be filled out every time and one part of that prescription goes to the government. What these guys were doing, or at least what they were forcing the pharmacists to do was to forge different doctors' names and patient information on the triplicate prescriptions. They likely would have been caught at some point when some sharp-eyed person in that government department saw too many prescriptions from a particular doctor and checked with that doctor. But until that happened they'd be making serious money selling those drugs on the street."

"Pretty smart ... I guess," I say.

Staff Sergeant Wheeler shakes his head. "They're not the brains of the outfit. Just a couple of punks doing what they're told and indulging their racist hate on the side. And when they were caught they were just like their pal, Lenny. Suddenly wanted to talk about how they didn't want to do it but they were forced to ... how they were threatened by their boss."

"Let me guess," Mia says, "No name—just a voice on a cell phone."

"Nope, not this time. They gave us a name. Guy named Richard Weston."

"A real guy?" Mia says.

"Uh-huh. Real guy. Long rap sheet in the U.S. and north as far as Vancouver. Some bad stuff along the way. Doesn't mind hurting people to get what he wants.

Either of you ever hear of this guy?"

"Richard Weston." I repeat the name, then shake my head. "Don't think I ever heard that name."

"Sounds more like a movie star's name than a bad guy," Mia says.

"Don't let the name fool you. He's bad, all right." Constable McCartney reaches into her briefcase again, pulls out another photograph, and holds it out to us. I'm looking at a big, bulky-looking guy with a beard that could use some work. I'm also looking at the meanest eyes I've ever seen. I stare at the photo for a long time.

"I wonder."

"Wonder what?"

I look up at the constable. "Have you shown this photo to Callie Snowden, the girl who lives at 624 Edmund Avenue? The night of the murder she saw a guy running out of the house. The person she described to me, well, I don't know, sounded something this guy."

Staff Sergeant Wheeler smiles at me. "The homicide detectives have already done that. She said she didn't get a great look at him that night. It was dark and he was heading out the door. But he did look back at her and she's all but certain it's him."

"Did she tell you that he tried to lure her to a meeting after that ... how he used Cal Krebs and a BS story about her dad wanting to see her?"

He nods. "She told us that too. And she mentioned you came to the rescue that night."

I shake my head. "I didn't do much."

"Yeah, you did." He looks over at Mr. Turley, then back at me. "Your principal's going to hate me saying this but you just might make it as a detective, after all." He chuckles before he says, "But I think we'd all prefer that you wait a few years, okay?"

"Okay. But there is one thing," I say. "If this Weston guy is still out there and if he thinks Callie can identify him ... I guess I just worry about how safe she is in that house."

Staff Sergeant Wheeler nods. "We've already got a BOLO out there and we're keeping an eye on 624 Edmund Avenue as well. Not round-the-clock but frequent drive-bys. We think we've got it covered."

I decide not to show off by telling Farhad and Mia that a BOLO is police-talk for "Be On the Lookout"—a bulletin or broadcast to all officers in a particular jurisdiction.

"Okay, one last question," I say.

The Staff Sergeant nods. "Shoot."

"Why are you telling us all this? Other than the corroboration thing."

"Everything we've told you here is either already public knowledge or will be soon ... other than the drive-bys at 624. And the truth is we felt that you three deserved to hear it from us. Sort of our way of saying thank you."

The officers stand up and shake hands with the three of us and Mr. Turley; then they're gone. I look at Mr. Turley to see if there's anything he wants to add to what's just been said.

He just smiles and says, "You better get back to class, okay?"

———————

I really am one of the great party planners, but I've got nothing on Callie. I figure that out in the first half-hour of her birthday bash. First of all, since that first time I saw her in the kitchen window of 624 Edmund Avenue, I have thought Callie is a beautiful girl. But this night she has taken beautiful to a whole new level. Her hair looks like the hair you see on those models in the ads on television, the ones where they shake their heads and their hair sort of dances.

Callie doesn't shake her head. She doesn't have to. She greets me at the door, takes my arm and reaches up to kiss me lightly, then leads me into the living room / dining room part of the house. I almost forget to give her the flowers and vase I bought for her. She takes them, tells me they're lovely, kisses me again and takes them into the kitchen.

"They'd get wrecked in here," she says as she returns. The place is wild. There are strobes pumping out flashes to the sound of a Drake song I can't remember the name of. There's a disco ball suspended from the centre of the living-room ceiling. It takes a minute for my eyes to adjust to the pulsing light.

When they do, I see that there are quite a few kids there already, some of them sitting on couches and chairs, others stretched out on the floor. I look around the room and realize I don't know most of the people there. I'm guessing they're Callie's friends from her school.

She introduces me and runs through the names; I remember maybe two. Farhad is there and he's sitting in a far corner with De-*bor*-ah Wong. He gets up, comes over to me and we do this sort of hand-jive greeting thing we've perfected since Farhad got back to being Farhad again. We think we're pretty cool but I notice a couple of the girls roll their eyes.

Mrs. Snowden comes into the room, greets me with a gentle hug and a great smile—I know where Callie's smile comes from.

"Nice to see you, Dom."

"Great to see you too, Mrs. Snowden."

She holds out a hand. "Car keys, please."

I pull out my keys although I'm not totally sure what's happening.

"You want to take the Satin Wagon for a spin?" I grin at her.

She shakes her head. "Uh-uh. Just making sure everyone's in shape to drive when the party's over. There's no alcohol here but I also know you're all teenagers and there might be those who bring some in. If you're okay to drive at the end of the night, you get your keys back; if not, I'm the chauffeur."

"That's okay with me," I tell her as she smiles again and heads off toward the kitchen. And it is. I like that

Mrs. Snowden doesn't actually come out and say no drinking; she's leaving it to us but if somebody does get a little sideways, at least they're not going to be driving.

"And while we're in confiscation mode," Callie grins, "I'll take your phone."

"What's this ... school?"

"Nope, but I don't want people staring at their phones instead of being in party mode."

I shrug and hand over my phone.

"How do you like the photo wall?"

I look where Callie is pointing and on one of the living room walls there's this white blanket for a background. And on a table right next to the background there are weird hats and a bunch of crazy fun stuff for props when people want to get their pictures taken. In fact, Farhad and Deborah are getting set up right now. Farhad's wearing a sombrero and pulling on a toga-looking thing and Deborah has donned a football helmet; she's smoking a cigar and holding a teddy bear.

"Hey, Dom, grab your phone and do the honours, okay?"

Callie hands me my phone. "Just for the pictures, then I take it back."

"Sure." I grin at Farhad as I head over there. "It's not every day I get to photograph a cross between a gaucho and a pharaoh."

"Ha ha."

"What about me?" Deborah says. "You gotta love my outfit."

"Deborah, you look exactly like I'd expect any girl who would date this guy to look."

We all laugh and I take a bunch of pictures of them in goofy poses and making faces. True to her word, Callie takes back the phone, and disappears, I'm guessing to stash it with all the other phones. She's back a few seconds later and takes hold of my arm again.

In the dining room, there's another person I don't know. He's older and he's the size of a boxcar. He's surrounded by computers and speakers.

"A deejay?" I look at Callie. "You hired a deejay? Wow."

She nods and beams at me and right on cue "Hot Tunes Haskins" (his name's on one of the speakers in very large glittery letters) rocks out Grace Ives's "Mirror." Callie guides me toward the centre of the room and we begin what we both know will be one of our last times together—maybe *the* last time. Farhad and Deborah

The Dark Won't Wait

285

are dancing too and pretty soon a bunch of people are up on the floor.

I happen to look over Callie's shoulder as the next guests are coming through the front door. It's Mia. She has a date and for a second I stop dancing and stare. Mia's date is Foster MacLennan.

I knew she kind of liked the guy but I'm still a little shocked when they walk into the party together. I turn with Callie so they won't know I've noticed them but as I do, Callie spots them and hauls me over to the door to greet the new arrivals.

Terrific.

I give Mia a hug and nod at Foster MacLennan who nods back at me. No smiles on either of our faces but I'm not about to wreck Mia's evening so I try to act like it's no big deal. My attention moves to something else anyway. Right behind Mia and her date is a guy in the brightest green jacket I've ever seen and he's carrying about ten pizzas.

Callie and her mom have a snacks table set up in the dining room on the opposite side of the room from Hot Tunes Haskins. On that table, there's cake, cookies, popcorn and smores. And now enough pizza to feed thirty teenagers. Or two of Hot Tunes Haskins. Hot Tunes looks pleased.

Some people grab pizza and a pop out of the cooler that's on the floor under the snack bar and we spend the next half-hour or so mingling, eating and dancing. I've just finished my second slice of pepperoni and green pepper when Callie announces it's Karaoke time.

She sets up a machine and microphone and for a few minutes people are pretty shy. Once again Farhad is first up. With the sombrero back in place, he performs a hilarious rendition of "Old Town Road." And for the next hour or so people take to the microphone, some pretty good, some worse than terrible.

And finally I muster all the courage I've got and head to the microphone for a turn. The truth is I've been practising and hoping maybe I'd get a chance to sing this song but now that the time is right, I don't know if I can do it and I certainly don't know that I can do it well.

But now that I have the microphone in my hand, I can't very well back down. The music starts and I don't really need to look at the lyrics. I know them by heart. The song is Ed Sheeran's "Perfect." My performance is a long way from perfect but I get through it and when

I'm finished I see tears in Callie's eyes. She moves to me and puts her arms around my neck.

From his corner spot, Farhad says, "You totally nailed it man." Which I know is a lie but it's what best friends are supposed to say. The room's pretty quiet for a couple of minutes after that.

Hot Tunes is getting ready to fire up the music and lights again but Mrs. Snowden beats him to the punch. She comes into the room and announces, "Bonfire's going pretty good if any of you want to head out into the backyard. I'm pretty sure you'll be able to hear the music from there." She turns and gives Hot Tunes a look that is somewhere between a smile and a grimace. "I guess we won't need the lights. The fire should take care of that."

I look at Callie. "Wow, a bonfire. You weren't kidding when you said this would be a party to remember. I'll remember it forever."

Everybody grabs more pizza and drinks and rolls out into the backyard. For a while, it's pretty quiet except for Haskins's tunes in the background. Some kids are toasting marshmallows and others are making smores, but most are just staring at the fire and enjoying the warmth of the night.

David A. Poulsen

Farhad tells the worst ghost story in the history of haunting but Foster MacLennan follows up with one that I have to admit is damn scary.

After maybe an hour and a half by the bonfire, the party is starting to wind down. Every part of it has been awesome. Callie and I have spent every minute of that hour and a half staying as close to each other as we can get.

Foster MacLennan and Mia are the first couple to leave. It's all I can do to keep from grabbing Mia by the arm and yelling at her that he's a creep and she should just stay here and I'll give her a ride home. But I don't do that.

As they're heading out the side gate leading from the backyard to the front, Callie says, "They're so nice."

"Yeah," I say through gritted teeth.

Hot Tunes Haskins packs up his equipment shortly after that and the rest of the group starts trickling away. Farhad and Deborah are the last to leave. Hugs and fist bumps. A half-hour later—it's around 1:30 in the morning—Callie and I are alone at the fire.

We sit and stare at the flames and think about stuff, maybe the same stuff—I don't know. I'm not sure how long we sit there but finally we douse the fire and head inside.

"I can help you clean up," I tell her. The stereo is playing a Taylor Swift *1989* and to be honest, it's a nice change from Hot Tunes Haskins.

Callie shakes her head. "Mom and I can do it in the morning." She picks up a note on the table. "From Mom." She reads out loud. "'Just ran out to the store to get some cleaner. Be back in fifteen.'" She smiles at me. "That's my mom's way of giving us a little time by ourselves."

"She's a cool lady."

Callie takes my hand. "We didn't get any pictures at the photo wall."

"You're right. But who's going to take them?"

"I thought ahead. We're going old school. Don't move." She points at the photo wall then runs downstairs and is soon back ... with a camera on a tripod.

"You stand right there and I'll set it on delay." She fusses and aims for a few seconds, then thinks of something.

She runs into the kitchen and is back in a few seconds carrying the vase with the flowers I'd brought her. She hands them to me. "I want them in the picture with us."

She steps to the camera, touches a switch and scoots up beside me.

David A. Poulsen

"Smile."

I put one arm around her and hold the vase in front of us. The flash goes off and she turns to me. "There's one more thing we haven't done yet tonight."

She slips her arms around my neck. I bend to her and our lips meet.

And that's when the lights go out.

26

JUNE 22–CONTINUED

Wait Until Dark

For a few seconds I'm thinking, *Wow, this girl goes all-out when she wants to make things romantic.* But then I realize the music is gone too. Which means the power is out. Except when I turn my head and look out the window I can see lights in other houses. So the power is out only in this house.

"Dom?" There's a tremble in Callie's voice and I can sense, even in the dark, that she's worried.

"Hey, no problem. I'll grab our phones and we can dial up the flashlights. Where did you put them?"

She doesn't get a chance to answer.

Because we're not alone.

"They're right here."

It's too dark to see much more than shapes but the

shape that just spoke those words is maybe eight metres away. It's a big shape and the voice sounds cold and dangerous. He flicks on one of the flashlights on one of the phones—I don't know if it's one of ours or his and then I realize it doesn't really matter.

There's a badass-sounding guy in the house with us and he's got the only light. In the glow of the phone's light I can see he also has a gun. And it's pointed at us.

The weird first thought that comes into my head as I look at the gun and the guy holding it is: *I wonder how long it takes to die from a gunshot wound.*

But a few seconds pass and he doesn't pull the trigger and I start to wonder if there's something else going on. I figure if we can get him talking and keep him talking maybe one of us will think of something.

"I'm betting you're Richard Weston." My voice is actually less shaky than I thought it would be.

He ignores me, focuses only on Callie.

"Where's your old man?"

"I don't know." Callie's voice is soft but firm. Neither of us wants to give this creep the satisfaction of thinking we're afraid of him.

"Bullshit, where is he?"

"Why did you kill Shane Krebs?" I say it mostly to get his attention off Callie and it works. He turns his eyes and the gun toward me.

"You open your mouth again, turd, and I'll put one in your brain." He raises the gun so that it's aligned exactly with my head and I'm pretty much convinced that he means exactly what he's saying.

I decide to shut up.

He turns just enough that he's looking at Callie again. Now the gun is aimed at her but at least he's lowered it so it's opposite her stomach.

"I'm not going to ask you again," he barks at her. "That bastard owes me money, a lot of money, and I want it. Now where is he?"

He moves one step closer to Callie and I decide I'm going to launch myself at him and hope for the best. One more step should bring him close enough for me to make a move. I try to will him to come just that little bit closer. *One step closer.*

I know that what I'm about to do is not going to work and is going to get me shot, maybe killed. But I can't just stand there and wait for this scumbag to murder us both without at least trying to do something about it.

Before he can take that one step, the night erupts in a very loud and incredibly awful noise. I'm not sure how to describe it except that it's close, or at least seems that way and the natural reaction is to plug your ears. It feels like the noise, whatever it is, is coming from the front steps of the house.

Weston doesn't plug his ears. But he is startled enough to make a half-turn in the direction of whatever made the noise. I take one step toward him and bring the vase down on the hand holding the gun. The vase shatters and Weston yells at the pain. He drops the gun and it skitters across the floor. I throw a wild punch and catch Weston on the shoulder. It's not a good punch and I know I haven't hurt him at all but while he's trying to turn back to us to throw a punch of his own, Callie grabs at his other hand, the one holding the phone. It too hits the floor. The flashlight goes out and in the instant dark that now surrounds us I can't see what's happened with the phone or the gun. The good news is Weston can't see anything either. The noise outside the house stops and is replaced by Weston yelling a lot of things that aren't particularly complimentary to Callie or me.

I'm about to dive across the floor and see if I can get

hold of the gun or maybe one of the phones when I feel a hand grab my arm. I know it's Callie and she's pulling me down the hall away from Weston. She guides me through the doorway into the kitchen and toward the back door.

Neither of us says anything, hoping that in the dark, Weston won't know where we are. I know the layout of the house well enough that I'm sure Callie's idea is that we'll escape out the back door before Weston can figure out where we are. I'm guessing he's scrambling around on hands and knees trying to find his gun or at least his phone.

"They're coming your way." His voice booms through the house.

Callie stops and I bump into her. Though we have to stay silent I'm betting she's doing the same thing I am—trying to gauge whether Weston is bluffing, that he's alone and there's no one at the back door. My guess is he's bluffing. But if I'm wrong and he actually does have someone posted there, things could get real ugly, real fast.

We're still in the kitchen but I can sense we're nearing the back of the house. I remember that there are two steps down to the small landing at the back door. And if you turn right there's a longer staircase leading back downstairs. Callie's still holding my hand and pulling me along. She slows and whispers, "Two steps down."

I start the shuffle-slide people use—at least I do, when I'm in the dark and I know there's something ahead. With Callie guiding me, I get down the two steps without breaking my neck and I can feel her beside me again. I can also feel that we're making that turn to the right.

"More stairs," she whispers again. Clearly she has decided not to risk trying the back entrance and running straight into Weston's accomplice if there is one. I'm about to argue but I feel myself losing my balance and I reach out to right myself. My hand makes contact with the railing that I remember runs the length of the staircase. I take hold as Callie urges and guides me down the stairs. We reach the bottom and for a few seconds I'm relieved not to have broken any bones in the process.

Despite the fact that most of the party took place in this part of the house, I'm pretty much a blank on the actual layout of the basement. Guess I wasn't really thinking about floor plans as Callie and I were slow-dancing to Sam Smith's "Too Good at Goodbyes."

Still Callie is leading the way and I'm more than happy to follow that lead. Finally we stop and I have a feeling she has led us into one of the downstairs rooms. I can hear her softly close a door.

"Furnace room," she whispers.

I actually nod my head before I remember she can't see me. She pulls me down so we're kind of huddled on the floor. I get it—she's trying to make us as small and invisible as possible. For a second I have one of those déjà-vu moments but I don't spend any time thinking about what the previous moment is that darted into and then out of my mind.

"We need a weapon," I whisper. It's weird trying to talk to someone who you know is right beside you but that you cannot see. Not a shadow, not a shape ... nothing. Except I can hear her breathing and mine, both of us almost panting like we'd just run a marathon ... but the rapid breathing isn't from exertion ... it's from fear.

"It's a furnace room," Callie says again and even in her whisper I can hear the frustration, the desperation. I wonder if she's thinking we should have taken our chances on the back door. I know that's what I'm thinking.

David A. Poulsen

Now we're trapped. And we've actually helped Weston because eventually he'll find us. He has to know we've come downstairs and there aren't that many rooms down here. I think there are a couple of bedrooms—Callie's and maybe one other. There's a bathroom and there's the furnace room. That's it—four places to look for us and even if the furnace room is the last place he looks, we're still maybe ten or fifteen minutes away from D-Day ... D as in Dead.

I have the weird déjà vu thing again and this time I know what it is I've seen before that triggers it. The play. *Wait Until Dark*. Specifically the time I got to rehearse the final scene in Suzy's apartment when I was playing the part of the evil Roat. There are similarities—the dark, a bad guy willing to do whatever it takes to force an innocent victim to give him the information he wants. And the victim—in this case, Callie—like Suzy, has the advantage of knowing her way around a place she's familiar with—even in the dark.

Of course, that advantage will disappear in a hurry if Weston finds his phone and the flashlight still works. He flicks it on, finds the gun and our chances of coming out of this alive are greatly reduced.

"Is there anything in here I can use on him?" I whisper in the direction I think Callie is located.

"I don't know. It's also the laundry room but I doubt if there's much ..."

For a second I wish I still had the vase. That thought is interrupted by a shout from upstairs. It's Weston. "Game's over, kiddies. I'm coming down. If you're smart you step out where I can hear you and you tell me what I want to know."

For a second all I can feel is panic. *Okay, deep breaths, just breathe deep,* I tell myself. *Just breathe* ... Whoa, wait a minute. He said, "...where I can hear you," not where I can see you. Either he didn't find his phone or the flashlight quit working when it hit the floor. Meaning he's in the dark. Advantage us.

Of course, what I don't know is if he has his gun but I'm betting he has. He wouldn't be coming down here without it. Even in the dark. *Especially* in the dark.

"We need to split up," I whisper and I barely get the words out when Callie squeezes my hand so hard I think she's going to break some bones.

"No ... no, don't leave me here. I can't—"

"Listen to me." It's hard to sound forceful when

you're whispering but I try anyway. "Listen to me. We'll have a better chance if we're not together. He can't see us and that's what we've got to use. It's all we've got."

"I don't want to be in here—"

I interrupt her again. "Can you get to one of those bedrooms on the other side?"

She doesn't answer.

"Get to one of those, get inside and close the door. But be ready. I'll distract him and when I do, you go for the stairs. I'll be right there with you. Keep going right out the front door no matter what. Even if he's got somebody else out there, we'll have a better chance than if we stay here. Remember the girl who went back upstairs to see what had happened after the shooting. Be that girl again. We can do this."

Another shout. "I'm coming down. I wouldn't try anything stupid, a-holes or I'll shoot you both dead as dirt."

"Go ... go!" I hiss at Callie. We stand up and ease our way to the door. I slowly open it, praying the hinges don't screech and tell him exactly where we are. They stay silent. I poke my head out and look toward where I think the stairs are. Nothing but darkness. I was right— he doesn't have light, so there's still a chance. If he's started down the stairs he's moving slowly and quietly.

I pull the door the rest of the way open and feel Callie let go of my hand. I can sense her moving out into the main part of the basement. Part of me wants to grab her and pull her back in here so we can at least be together at the end. But I don't.

Instead I hold my breath and hope she's crossing the floor to one of the other rooms. I'm guessing she'll choose her bedroom. It might have been a good idea to confirm that before she left but it's a little late now.

"When I get there you'll have exactly five seconds to tell me what I want to know."

From the sound of Weston's voice I'm guessing he's about halfway down the stairs. Moving slowly, probably because he doesn't know how many stairs there are and whether we'll be waiting at the bottom ready to hit him with something. Which wouldn't be a bad idea if I actually had something to hit him with.

"If you don't, you'll both die and I'll get the information another way."

I start feeling around the walls and floor to see if there might be something I can use. As great as a five-iron would be, it's not likely that many people keep their

David A. Poulsen

golf clubs in the furnace/laundry room. *If* Callie or her mom even play golf. There are shelves along one wall and I feel my way along each shelf. Detergent, fabric softener sheets, a stack of towels, nothing even remotely useful as a possible weapon. No tools, no lengths of pipe, not even a chunk of rubber hose ... nothing.

I'm about to give up on that when my hand comes up against something a little more solid than towels or fabric softener. At first I'm not sure what it is but as I run both hands over the object I finally decide it feels like a trophy of some kind. Maybe 30 centimetres high, just about the width of my hand at the base with some kind of statue on top. You can't be very proud of a trophy you won if it winds up sharing a shelf with laundry detergent. A crazy thought to have but this whole thing is crazy.

I lift it and it feels pretty good in my hand. Heavier than plastic. The problem is I'd have to be really close to Weston to use it on him. Close enough that even in the dark, he'd be able to put a bullet into me. Unless I can somehow get behind him which might be hard to pull off.

Anyway the trophy's all I've got so I take it from the shelf, hoping like hell I don't have to use it. I'm sure Weston has reached the bottom of the stairs by now and I move in behind the door. It's not much of a hiding place but it's the best I can do. If the man is dumb enough to walk into the laundry room and just keep walking I can bring the trophy down on his head. It probably wouldn't knock him out but it might buy Callie enough time to get up the stairs.

Might.

"We can do this the easy way or we can do it the hard way. Doesn't matter a damn to me." Weston's voice is closer now; he's reached the bottom of the stairs and is in the basement. The one thing we've got going for us is he doesn't know the layout—where the rooms are or even how many there are. More shades of *Wait Until Dark*. Now if I can just muster the same courage Suzy had when the time comes. And that's the part I can't guarantee. Because the truth is I've never been more scared in my life and what I want to do most of all is curl up in a little ball on the floor and just hope and pray he won't find me.

"I'll tell you what you want to know." Callie's voice stuns me back to reality.

What the hell is she doing? I'm the one who's supposed to be doing the distracting. I can't see her but her voice tells me she's almost directly across from me. A door closes. I assume it's the door to her bedroom but is she going in or coming out. *Where is she?*

"Move out into the centre of the room, both of you." Weston's voice sounds a little more confident. Maybe *over*-confident. And stupid. In the total darkness how is he going to know if we're in the centre of the room or in two opposite corners? He answers that one quickly.

"And I want you both talking ... starting now."

On the other side of the basement a door closes. Loudly. Again I try to guess whether that signifies Callie going into or out of a room. But I have no way of knowing. Just as I don't know what her idea was in closing the door and making sure Weston heard it.

Is she trying to draw him over there? Silence follows the noise of the door closing and I'm guessing Weston is wondering that same thing.

Several long seconds pass before he says again, "I want to hear you. Start talking."

I get a sense from the sound of his voice that he's moving slowly toward the other side of the basement—toward the door that closed a few seconds ago. I ease the door of the furnace room open—ready to make my move.

"Okay, I'm right here," Callie says and that starts my heart pounding even harder than it had been already.

She has to be setting him up for me; it's the only thing that makes sense. But what exactly is she expecting me to do? I think about tackling him but if I charge across the room and miss him in the dark, things could go very badly. I'm still trying to decide what my best course of action is when Weston's voice breaks my concentration.

"Put your hand out."

"What for?" Callie's voice is softer but she doesn't sound scared.

"Just do it." Weston's voice is very different, almost a growl. "Put your hand out so I know exactly where you are."

"Okay ... okay."

It's time. I crouch and set my body to propel myself at the last sound I heard from Weston. I've decided to take his advice. I have my hand out. I figure if I can get a feel for where he is, I'll bring the trophy down on his head. For a second I hesitate, afraid I could miss him altogether and hit Callie. But if I do nothing that's worse.

Just as I start my charge across the basement, there's a bright flash that lights up the room for a split

David A. Poulsen

second. The flash is blinding but before the darkness settles over the room again, I make out the hulking, scary shadow that is Weston. He's just a few short steps from Callie, his back to me. The bad news is that he now knows exactly where she is. The good news is that he has no idea where I am. The darkness seems even more overpowering in the instant or two after the vivid, searing light. I move as fast as I dare.

Right there, I tell myself. *He's there, he's right there.*

I swing the trophy, using about the same motion I use in throwing home to beat the base runner. Occasionally my throw is off-line. I pray that this is not.

I feel the solid crunch of the trophy's heavy base as it makes contact with the back of Weston's head. He yells out his pain in the form of a string of curses. My forward motion carries me into him and I can feel him go down. What I don't know is if I've hurt him enough to give us time to escape.

"Come on!" I yell at Callie. "Come on!"

There's a couple of seconds when it feels like nothing is happening and I'm afraid she's stumbled over him and he's got hold of her. But then she's there. Our hands find each other and we bolt for the stairs. She takes the lead again and I'm good with that. She knows the way better than I do and we're only going to get one chance at this.

"Hold it right there!" Weston yells, and I can tell, again from the direction of his voice, that he's still on the floor, either lying down or maybe sitting up. I'm hoping I at least slowed him down.

Callie hits the stairs running and I stumble, almost go down, then right myself.

The gunshot is louder than I expected a gunshot to be, maybe because it's inside the house. I feel something in my hand, the hand Callie isn't holding—it's something hot and really heavy. And it hurts like hell. There's another shot and a thud into the wall near us.

We reach the top of the stairs and Callie turns us away from the back door. We're going out the front door. I'm not a guy who prays much but I whisper a quick prayer right there that Weston doesn't have a partner out there waiting for us.

I can hear Weston. He's coming up the stairs. He's groaning and cursing, a weird and scary mix of almost animal sounds. We've got a decent head start but a bullet travels a long way in a short time. We've got to go faster. Callie's hauling on my arm to get me to move quicker and I'm trying, but when you're moving fast in the dark there's this feeling that you're about to run into something or fall over something and your legs will only allow you to go a certain speed and no faster.

And there's something else. I suddenly feel kind of weird—sort of light-headed. Like I'm off balance or something. As we get to the front door, my hand is now throbbing with major pain and for the first time I wonder if I've been shot. I tell myself that makes no sense and that I must have done something to it when I hit Weston with the trophy.

Callie propels us through the front door and out onto the porch. It's amazing coming from the total darkness inside the house to the semi-darkness outside—with streetlights here and there and a little light from a few of the houses—it's like a sunny afternoon in July. I feel energized again and Callie and I are down the steps and onto the sidewalk, both of us running hard.

That's when it hits me. Mrs. Snowden took my car keys when I arrived. Going back in to look for them isn't an option. We have to run and hope we can get far enough ahead of Weston to not get shot. And even as I'm thinking it, I'm also thinking we have zero chance of pulling that off. We get to the main sidewalk and skid to a stop.

"My car keys are—"

"I know."

Both of us are panting for breath and both of us know we have to keep moving. Which way do we go? I start to the right; Callie starts to the left which would have been a funny moment if there wasn't a killer a few seconds from bursting out of the house, gun blazing. Panic is starting to set in and for the second time a dizzy spell hits me.

"We have to ... hide." I have trouble getting the words out.

"Where? There's no place to ..."

She doesn't finish the sentence. There's a roar to our left and I look that way. Coming hard is a car, its horn blaring—no, not a horn, but a noise, loud, almost painful as it blares its chaos of sound and confusion. I've heard it before but I'm having trouble making sense of things. As the car screams to a stop at the curb, the passenger door swings open.

"Get in!" The driver screams it, then again. "Hurry up. Get in!"

Callie's the first to move. She dives across to the middle and I follow her in. I look over at the driver.

Foster MacLennan.

I grab Callie's arm and start to pull her back out of the car.

"You do that and you're both dead!" Foster MacLennan yells. "Trust me, he'll kill you and he won't give it a second thought."

Trust me? Are you kidding me? You're as bad as Weston. But before I can voice the thought, Callie pulls her arm away from me.

"We're going ... now!"

I look up at the house. The door's still open and I can see a shadow inside staggering toward the door.

I look back, first at Callie, then at Foster MacLennan who's revving his engine.

"Go!" I yell. "Let's go!"

McLennan jams the gas pedal to the floor and we scream away from the curb, tires squealing, the powerful engine destroying what's left of the peaceful quiet of the night. We move ahead so fast and so hard that the passenger door slams shut from the force of the motion.

Turns out it's a good thing that happened because as

I reach my hand out to pull it shut, I realize I'm not going to be able to do that. My hand is limp and drenched in blood.

"That bastard shot me." The words sound slurred like I'm drunk or something.

As we race off into the night, for the third time in the last few minutes, I feel weak and woozy. But this time I can't shake it off and seconds later, I feel myself falling into unconsciousness.

And there's nothing I can do about it.

27

JUNE 23

The After Party

There are four people in the room when I wake up.

Callie is sitting to the left of the bed holding my hand, the one that doesn't hurt. Mom and a guy in a white smock are on the right side of the bed. And at the far end of the bed, Foster MacLennan is leaning against the wall, doing his *Breakfast Club* impersonation again.

At least it feels like my brain is back to normal. And I have questions, a lot of questions.

The guy in the smock is the first to speak. "Welcome back," he says. He's wearing a name tag that says *Dr. Adam Reddick*. "How are you feeling, Dom?"

I look up at him. Young guy, tall, dark hair, kind of a smile. "Okay I guess," I tell him. "What about my hand. I play baseball and ..."

The Dark Won't Wait

313

He shakes his head.

"Afraid you'll have to miss the playoffs this year. The good news? No structural damage. My guess is you'll be ready to go for next season." The smile gets bigger. I like the guy.

I look over at Callie. "What happened after I ... after I ..."

"Fainted," Foster MacLennan says with a smirk.

"Passed out," Callie corrects him.

We all look at Dr. Reddick. He says, "Lost consciousness."

"Yeah, that," I say.

"I'll let you have that discussion after I'm gone," the doctor says. "Everything's good here but I'd like you to just rest a little longer and the nurse will come in and change your bandage. Then you can go home." He glances at his watch. "Maybe a half-hour or so." He looks at Mom. "Bring him in next week and I'll take another look at the hand, but everything's looking good. No fist fights, okay?" He pats my shoulder and heads out.

Everybody looks at everybody else for a minute or two. I have ten thousand questions I want to ask. For starters I can't believe that Foster MacLennan is standing at the end of my hospital bed. I turn my head to look at Callie.

"What's he doing here?"

"He was driving the getaway car, remember? If it wasn't for him, you and I might have a few more bullet wounds to worry about."

My mind flashes back to those few seconds in front of 624 Edmund Avenue: Weston about to stumble out onto the porch, gun in hand and in a really bad mood. Sirens in the distance, coming closer but not soon enough to keep Weston from shutting up Callie and me permanently. And the car, engine wailing, tires screaming, slamming to the curb in front of us, the passenger door swinging open and the driver yelling at us to get in.

Foster MacLennan.

"I thought you were one of them," I say.

He shrugs, doesn't say anything. Messing with me. I'm not about to beg so I look up at Callie who hasn't let go of my hand since I woke up.

She smiles at Foster MacLennan and says, "Come on. Tell him what you told us." I notice Mom is smiling too. So everybody's in on the big secret but me.

Foster MacLennan actually manages to straighten up, but only for a second. He leans on the rail thing at the end of my bed. He smiles at Callie and Mom but his face becomes a whole lot less friendly when he looks at me.

"The Krebs brothers are my cousins," he says. "I've grown up with them around me all the time. Since I was a little kid, they were at our house for Christmas dinners and the odd summer barbecue. For a while it was okay; we'd hang out at the playground or the swimming pool when we were young. But pretty soon they were getting into trouble. Creepy stuff. Bullying other kids, shoplifting, a few break-and-enters, hurting animals ..."

I think about the cat, Bernie, in Farhad's locker.

"One time they beat up this old guy who was walking his dog. Kicked the crap out of the old man and the dog. Took his wallet. They got sixteen bucks." He shakes his head.

"And then it was drugs. At first they were just smoking some weed. Then they figured out there was money in dealin' the stuff. From weed, they graduated to other big-time stuff, making a fair amount of money." He stands up and stretches, then leans on the rail again.

"About a year ago, they hooked up with a couple of

David A. Poulsen

other guys. One of them was Weston and the other was Callie's dad." He looks at Callie. "I just found out that part tonight—the part about your dad."

"That was about the time Shane and Jackie Krebs moved into our house," Callie says.

Foster McLennan looks at her and nods. "Weston was a big-time badass. Scared the hell out of me. And I'm pretty sure he scared the crap out of my cousins and your dad too."

He looks back at me. "It wasn't long before they started the thing with the prescription drugs. It was Weston's idea but it was Shane and Jackie who did the scamming and Callie's dad who sold the stuff on the street. But Shane and Jackie were stupid, not giving Weston his full share. You don't screw around with a guy like that. It got Shane killed and I'm guessing Callie's dad thought he was next. Even if he wasn't in on stealing from Weston, if Weston *thought* he was, that would be enough to get Mr. Snowden a spot on cemetery hill. And then Weston decided that Callie could be a witness against him and started talking about how she was next. Only thing is, he never figured she'd be back living in her old house, must have just found that out in the last few days, was waiting for the right time. Tonight was the right time."

It took a minute or so to take in all he'd just said. "How do you know all this stuff?"

He shook his head. "When you said before that you thought I was one of them, you were right. Early on I got in on a couple of sales of weed and even some crack. I liked the money but I hated everything else about it. But they had me. When I said I wanted out they told me they'd make sure the cops knew all about me. And they told me they'd hurt my little sister." His voice drops down as he says that last part.

"So I said I'd keep doing stuff but that I'd only drive for them. They know I'm pretty good at that so they said okay."

"Foster's a race car driver," Callie says. "He told us about that while you were still sleeping."

Foster MacLennan shakes his head. "Just amateur stuff. And that's *all* I do for them. Like the night Shane and Cal and Lenny Purvis did the number on Shirvani's drug store, I was waiting outside. In the truck, ready to go.

"You were their driver but that's all." I have a little trouble with that.

He shrugs. "I don't really care if you believe it or not.

That's how it was. They thought they were cool having their own driver. Like a chauffeur. And I was fine with it too. At least I wasn't dealing. And that's how I spotted you, knew you were following us. Which is why I jumped you that day. If those guys had found out what you were up to, you'd have been dead inside of a day, trust me."

I can see that part of the story is news to Callie and my mom.

"So what about tonight? Did you know Weston was going to try to get to Callie?"

He shakes his head. "I was taking Mia home and I saw him and his Camaro parked a block away ... watching. I knew he must have figured out that Callie was back in that house and he had some plan to get to her. I dropped Mia off and came back. But his car was gone. I cruised the street a couple of times but I didn't see him. I figured he must have taken off."

Callie interrupts him. "This is my favourite part of the story."

But it has to wait. The nurse comes into the room wheeling a tray with some medical supplies on it. She doesn't say a lot and has the bandage changed in a couple of minutes. She smiles at me, I thank her and she wheels the tray back out of the room. I look expectantly at Foster MacLennan waiting for him to go on with the story.

He grins. "I was going past the house for what I figured was the last time and I saw the lights go out. I figured you two must be getting down to some serious makin' out and I thought just for laughs I'd give the old horn a blast just to mess you up."

I think about what he's saying. "That god-awful noise ..."

His grin turns into a laugh. "Yeah, that's my horn. I have it programmed to play a Black Sabbath guitar riff at probably a few more decibels than are actually legal. Callie tells me my timing was pretty good. Pretty lucky."

"Lucky? That was a damn miracle." And for the first time Foster MacLennan and I are laughing together.

"I was laughing so hard as I drove away from the house, I almost didn't see his car. But there it was in a driveway in the next block, tucked in behind a pickup. I could see he wasn't in the car so I figured he was either watching the house deciding when to make his move or he was already in there. I called the cops and then I decided to park about half a block away and be ready if there was something I needed to do. I was going to wait fifteen minutes and if the cops weren't there by then I'd go to the door, make sure you two were okay. It was seven minutes in when you came running out of the house. I knew you weren't out there to enjoy the night air. So I thought I'd see if you wanted a ride."

He's grinning again. I hope nobody is going to say something like, "Foster MacLennan saved your lives." I was very glad he showed up when he did but I didn't really want to go through life thinking I owed my life to a guy I still wasn't sure I liked.

"Weston ... did the cops—?"

Callie interrupts me with a smile and a nod. "Oh, yeah, they got him. They were just a minute or two behind Foster. They just left a few minutes ago. Questioned all of us. They said they'd be talking to you later."

I look at Foster. "One thing I don't get. Why did Cal continue to work with Weston after he'd killed Cal's brother?"

"Simple motivation. It's called fear. Weston's a scary dude. Cal didn't want to be the next dead body."

For once I have no trouble agreeing with Foster MacLennan.

Mom steps up to the bed for the first time. "I'd say

that's about a half-hour. I think we better get Callie home. She called her mom earlier so Mrs. Snowden knows all about what happened tonight. But she might like to see her daughter sooner rather than later. And I have a feeling we could all use a little sleep."

I sit up in bed, glad I'm still in my own clothes and not one of those hospital gown things. I'm a little dizzy and my hand hurts but I'm feeling okay. As I stand up, Foster MacLennan says, "Sleeping Beauty's already had a nice nap. It started right after he fainted."

"Lost consciousness," I correct him.

"Right," he laughs. We bump fists and I take Callie's hand as we head for the door. I have no idea what time it is but as I look out the hospital room window I can see that the stillness and blackness of a dark, dark night are starting to fade. Dawn's first light is just appearing on the eastern horizon.

When we reach the main floor of the hospital, Farhad is waiting. He looks like he hasn't had a lot of sleep. I have no idea how long he's been sitting there but I suspect it's a while. When he sees us he stands up, comes forward and gives me a hug.

"Glad you're okay, man. They said you had all the

visitors allowed so I thought I'd just wait."

"I appreciate that, Farhad, I really do. You're the best."

He grins at me. "You might be right."

Then he looks at Foster. "I heard you helped out."

Foster shrugs. "A little maybe, no big deal."

"Cool," Farhad says.

There's a moment where neither of them says anything. Foster smiles and nods a little nod.

Maybe my head's still a little fuzzy but I have this thought—make that a few thoughts. There was a time not very long ago when I thought Hastings High was just a place where people learned math and social and English. And they ate lunch in the cafeteria and they acted in plays or played for the basketball team. And a few of them sat on a bench before and after school and talked about stuff.

But now I realize there's so much more. There's bad and good. Not just at Hastings but at every school. And it's better if I'm aware of the reality. I can't change the world but I at least need to know it needs changing.

We walk out of the hospital into the spreading red dawn.

28

JULY 3

Farewell to the Girl in the Window

Callie and her mom left this morning. I'm standing outside the terminal at the International Airport. A few minutes ago, I watched their plane take off, make a wide turn and head southwest over the city and in the direction of Vancouver Island.

I'm glad I'm by myself so nobody can see the tears.

Callie and I have talked a lot since the night of the party and everything that happened after. Her dad was arrested in Phoenix, Arizona and will be tried in the fall sometime.

We agreed that it would be just about impossible for us to be boyfriend/girlfriend while we're living hundreds of kilometres from each other. Even with Skype, Zoom, Facetime and all that stuff, there's nothing that comes

David A. Poulsen

close to being with one another. Isn't there a Bruce Springsteen song called "Human Touch?"

So now what? I guess life goes on. School will start up in the fall. Farhad and Mia and I will meet at the bench and talk about the day and each other and all the women who are crazy about Farhad. We won't talk much about school.

And I don't think we'll talk much about all the stuff that happened through the spring. None of us will forget any of it but I doubt that we'll want to talk about it all that much. I know I won't.

A few days ago Farhad and I were eating French fries and drinking Cokes at Vinnies. Out of the blue Farhad said, "You and me, we're not the same people we were a few months ago."

That was it. He didn't say anything else and I didn't really have an answer right then so we went back to our fries. But he was right. A few months ago I didn't have my own car, I hadn't seen a girl in a window and I hadn't been caught up in a drug-related murder case. And the racism thing—I'm still trying to get my head around it—how ugly it is, and how it's hurt my best friend. I guess it's not surprising that we're not who we were before all that.

I look at my watch. Farhad and Mia are taking me to a racetrack this afternoon to watch Foster MacLennan race. I think it's supposed to get my mind off Callie leaving. That won't happen but it should be an okay time.

Callie and her mom have been in the air for about ten minutes. I wonder if she's read it yet. I gave her an envelope just before she went through the boarding gate. It's funny—neither of us liked the idea of being just friends. Or at least we didn't want to *say* that's what we would be. It seems like so much less than what we want to be.

But maybe being friends will be okay—maybe not today, maybe not right now. Mom said that sometimes love triumphs over what seems like impossible odds. And she could be right. But even if that doesn't happen, I know I'll never forget Callie Snowden, my first real girlfriend.

Girl.

Friend.

What I put in the envelope was a verse from the poem, "Elegy Written in a Country Churchyard" that we studied in English this year. It was one of my favourite parts of the whole school year. And in this verse, it felt

David A. Poulsen

like Thomas Gray had found the perfect words for what I wanted Callie to know. I hope he doesn't mind my borrowing them.

> *Large was his bounty, and his soul sincere,*
> *Heav'n did a recompense as largely send:*
> *He gave to Mis'ry all he had, a tear,*
> *He gain'd from Heav'n ('twas all he wish'd) a friend.*

ACKNOWLEDGMENTS

Books don't just happen because an author decides to sit down and write one. At least my books don't happen that way. There are people who contributed to this book, lots of them without any idea that they were doing that. Special thanks to the Bozeman Actors Theatre and Kari Doll who directed that company's 2020 production of *Wait Until Dark*. Kari's generous sharing of a behind-the-scenes look at that production was beyond helpful. To the management and staff of Radio City Music Hall in New York City who facilitated my falling in love with a movie that remains one of my favourites even after all these years. To Grant Reddick, my high school drama teacher, who nurtured my love of theatre and who remains a cherished friend to this day. To the Canada

David A. Poulsen

Council for the Arts—I acknowledge the support of an independent artist grant that enabled this writing to take place. To Bev Brenna, my brilliant and kind editor who has been a joy to work with. To my granddaughter Chloe. It's been a long time since I attended a teenager party. And—who would have guessed—they've changed a little. The party that takes place in the latter stages of this book was created and choreographed by Chloe. And for another granddaughter, Gabriella. There is a lot of Mia in Gabriella or maybe there's a lot of Gabriella in Mia.

David A. Poulsen

AUTHOR INTERVIEW

Which came first, the characters or the plot? Was this one always intended to be a mystery/thriller? And what were some of the steps taken and decisions made along the way? Is it true that crafting a plot for mysteries and thrillers is more complicated than plotting in other genres?

Most, if not all, of my books start with characters. I try to write characters that interest me, that I care about and that readers will care about, and then, particularly in mystery/thrillers I try to put them in situations (plot) that they have to work their way out of. Yes, I wanted to write a murder mystery for teen readers partly because it was my favourite genre as a kid (and still is) and partly because so many young adult readers that I have spoken with have expressed their love of mysteries as well. More complicated? I'm not sure. I am not an outliner. I prefer to sit down and write and work out the plot points as I go. That might be a little more difficult with mysteries but I want to find out the answers at the same time as my "detective(s)" do, rather than having everything worked out for them ahead of time.

Thrillers are well-suited to theatrical projects, and this one works on the landscape of Knott's play, *Wait Until Dark*, and its subsequent film. How did this backdrop become a muse for your writing, and what do you see as some major differences between your work and the original story (other than the fact that a book is a book, and a film is a film ...)?

I saw the movie *Wait Until Dark* at Radio City Music Hall in New York City and loved it. One of the truly suspenseful films I have ever seen. What I wanted to do was create a final scene as suspenseful as the one in the play and movie. Then it seemed like a cool idea to actually bring *Wait Until Dark* into this story and that allowed me to write scenes involving theatre which is a longtime passion of mine. I have to say that I had more fun writing this book than almost any book I've written to date.

Audrey Hepburn and Alan Arkin star in the film version of *Wait Until Dark*. Are there stars you would select to play in leading roles if your book morphs someday into movie territory?

Such a great question but the truth is I just don't know enough of today's teen stars to offer an intelligent answer. I wouldn't mind if Jennifer Anniston was in the movie somewhere but that's mostly because I have a crush on her—probably not a great reason to cast someone in the film ... although Jennifer as Dom's mom? Hmmm.

Many authors talk about how their own life experiences often create underpinnings for their writing endeavours. What's in your past that rose to the occasion in this project, helping you through aspects of characterization, setting, and/or scene work?

I grew up wanting to be an actor and even went to New York to study theatre. I realized early on that I had neither the talent nor the temperament to be an actor, and it was at about that same time that I realized that writing was the creative endeavour I wanted to devote my life to. But I still love theatre. So to write a murder mystery that includes two of the things I care most about—theatre and baseball—is a definite win for me.

This story has some serious themes, including racism and racist hate crimes. How are your connections to schools helping keep you current where contemporary life meets fiction? Or are the themes you have included been part of your long-term knowledge of local schools and communities?

First of all, I am so fortunate that my writing has paved the way for me to have made school visits across Canada as well as in the United States, Japan and South Korea. And one of the things I make a point of doing is listening to the students in those schools from elementary to high school. I do that for a couple of reasons—first because I want my young characters to sound like the kids of today sound. It's important to me to get their voice right. And secondly, I want to know what kids in schools are talking about—what matters to them, what they think is wrong with the world around them, and what is right about that world too. Today's kids are smart, they care about important things and they have well-thought-out things to say about them.

What are your hopes for this title, now that it's completed?

As with all of my books I hope that readers are intrigued by the characters and entertained by the story. And while I don't set out to teach lessons I do hope that having the central characters face the evil of racism might at least get my readers thinking and talking about that unfortunate part of the world we live in (though I know many are already doing that). Oh, and I wouldn't mind earning $100,000 or so in royalties!!

What advice do you have for young writers interested in crafting their own new titles?

First, read. For your enjoyment but also because surrounding yourself with books and stories written by people who love what they do and are good at it is an important step in becoming a writer. I write because I loved the stories and books I consumed when I was growing up. I so admired the people who could create those stories and I wanted to see if I could do it too.